ORDINARILY SARAH

ORDINARILY SARAH

BOOK II: RELENTLESS

SARAH ELIZABETH ROSE

LitPrime
"Your story is our priority"

LitPrime Solutions
East Brunswick Office Evolution
1 Tower Center Boulevard, Ste 1510
East Brunswick, NJ 08816
www.litprime.com
Phone: 1-800-981-9893

Published by LitPrime Solutions: 02/05/2025

ISBN: 979-8-88703-450-8(sc)
ISBN: 979-8-88703-451-5(e)

Library of Congress Control Number: 2024924971

CONTENTS

PART III: LETTERS FROM SARAH TO HER FAMILY AND CLOSE FRIENDS

Also by Sarah Elizabeth Rose
Ordinarily Sarah (Ambassador International, 2016)

This book is for my husband. He
lived through it with me. He
kept me sane. He comforted me
after the nightmares came.
He jostled my memory when my
memory needed to be jostled.
He helped me move forward when
I did not think it was
possible to move at all. He assured
me there was hope when
I had given up all hope. He prayed
for me without ceasing.

PREFACE

MY FIRST BOOK, *Ordinarily Sarah*, took out all my insides: physically, mentally, emotionally, and spiritually. I was turned inside out, and I never thought I could write again. Ever. I was finished.

But the people who read *Ordinarily Sarah* soon began to clamor for more.

"What happened to you afterward, Sarah? What happened to your daughter and her husband and their five kids? Tell us, Sarah. Write it down. We want to know."

"And you never told us how you survived those terrible years when your daughter and her family were held as prisoners. Twenty years they were gone. And you never heard one word from them in all that time?"

"Later, after they all escaped, you never told us what happened to them. When did they come out? How did they come out? How are they coping in their brand-new world?"

"Tell us, Sarah. We want to know. We all have had terrible things happen in our lives. When those terrible things happen, how can we survive? Can we look to your writings? Can we, perhaps, learn something from you?"

"We all have dark days. How do we get to the other side of those days? How do we find the light when the sky turns black and the sun, moon, and stars have all fallen down? How can we live when our lives are so broken that no one can put us together again? When our lives look like Humpty Dumpty, and all the king's horses, and all the king's men can't put humpty together again. Tell us how you did it, Sarah."

"How did you get past the nightmares and the daymares. How did you get past the sadness so deep it could not be measured?"

"And the betrayals.
The broken promises.
The blank stares.
The rolling eyes.
The feeling that you must be insane."
"Tell us Sarah. Tell us please.
We think you can help us."

Dear readers,

I will tell you the story, then, of what happened next. I will tell you some things that should have been in the first book but were not. And I will tell you how I survived.

Many years ago, after the judge told us we could not see our daughter and family unless they initiated contact with us, we were done. We knew they would never initiate contact with us. Ever. We were dead to them. And so we put all of them to rest. There was nothing more we could do. We had to accept the fact that we would never see them again. Ever. It was over. And I did not know how I would survive.

Until one day, my sweet eight-year-old granddaughter (not involved in the cult) told me this: "Don't give up, Grandma! Never ever give up! Don't quit until it is done!"

And right then and there, I realized that my granddaughter needed me. The rest of my family needed me. I had to figure out a way to survive. And so I did. I began to move forward. Haltingly. But determined. Despite the thorn of great sorrow embedded in my flesh. Despite the Darkness that had enveloped me. Despite the gnawing inside of me that reminded me every single day that my daughter and her family had vanished. Despite the fact there was nothing more I could do to get them out.

Somehow, I figured out a way to get to the other side. Past the Wolf at my door, huffing and puffing, trying to blow my life apart. Past the Spiders spinning at their webs, trying to entrap my mind. Past the Owllike Creatures flying down from the heavens and trying to take away my soul. Past the losing of everything, including the life I had once lived as "Ordinarily Sarah." I could no longer live as ordinary Sarah had lived. My life would never again be ordinary.

Come with me then, dear readers, and I will share the rest of my story. Not because I want to write it. But because I might be able to help you. I will write it down for you.

The Dark Angel took away everything.
She took away my child,
She took away my grandchild,
She took away five of my grandchildren to come.
She took away my work,
And my purpose for life.
She took away my joy,
And the tears that would never fall.
She took away sleep at night,
And peace at daybreak.
She took away my family,
And my family to be.
She took away my memories,
And the present,
And the future to dream dreams of.
She took away color and light.
She took away laughter.
She took away pieces of my heart,
And slices of my soul.
She took away the world as I once knew it,
And she took away my courage to rebuild it.
Most terrible of all,
She almost took away my faith.
And she nearly took away,
God.
—*Ordinarily Sarah*

The dark angel took away everything.
(Photo by Donna Lark)

During our earthly journeys, sometimes we find ourselves in the wilderness. Alone. Living in empty houses—or in no houses at all. Or in anything at all. Living in nothingness.

Our Lord Jesus lived in the wilderness of a desert for forty days. And while living in that desert, Jesus was tempted by the devil. The devil offered Jesus food because he had none. He offered Jesus power and authority over all the nations of the world. He challenged Jesus to prove he was the Son of God. But Jesus, even though famished and alone, would have none of it. Jesus did not give in to the devil's temptations. And after surviving being subjected to the devil's poorly veiled lies for forty days, Jesus began his earthly ministry.

Later in his life, Jesus spent three days in another kind of wilderness. The first day on a cross. The second in hell. And the third day back to life, leaving his grave clothes behind in his tomb. None of us knows exactly what happened during that time when Jesus was in the wilderness, but we do know that while Jesus was hanging on his cross, there was a moment when he thought his Father had forsaken him. And in that moment, Jesus brought comfort to all of the rest of us. Even our Lord Jesus had a moment of questioning. Just like us. And God always understands.

My God, my God, why have you forsaken me?
(Matthew 27:46 ESV)

Some of us spend short periods of our lives in the wilderness. Others of us may spend our entire lifetimes in the middle of dry and dusty places. Some of God's people of long ago spent seventy years in a place called Babylon. Seventy years away from their homes! How could that be? But it was. And while they were there, God wanted—even expected—them to survive. God instructed his people to build houses, plant gardens, marry, and live in peace. And they did. God promised to bring them back to their homeland one day. And God kept his promise.

> *For thus says the Lord: When seventy years are completed for Babylon, I will visit you, and I will fulfill to you my promise and bring you back to this place. For I know the plans I have for you, declares the Lord, plans for welfare and not for evil, to give you a future and a hope. (Jeremiah 29:10–11 ESV)*

God is always near to us. No matter what our wilderness looks like or how long it lasts. And when the time is right, he brings us home.

We have hope. And we have a future.

Still, it can be difficult while we are located in an unfamiliar place. For some of us, our experiences are not unlike the experiences the characters had in *The Wizard of Oz*. In this tale, a young girl named Dorothy finds herself in the middle of a fierce tornado, and when the dust finally settles, she finds herself in a strange land. A land full of wicked witches, deep forests, flying monkeys, talking trees, a fearful scarecrow, a rusty tin man, and a very cowardly lion. But even though the witches are frightening, the flying monkeys are terrifying, and the talking trees are horrifying, Dorothy remains hopeful as she follows the path to see a wizard, accompanied by her odd, but kind trail-mates.

Dorothy had found herself in a wilderness, in a new world that was dangerously tilting, nearly lying on its side, and sometimes as dark as the night sky, with neither moon nor stars. And her new world was filled with scary things. But she and her friends stuck together and forged their way past all the dangers of the forest and all of the curses from the mouth of a wicked witch. Finally, the wicked witch was destroyed, Dorothy and her friends found the wizard, and Dorothy was able to go home by simply clicking together her ruby red shoes.

Dorothy was brave. So were her friends. We need to be brave too when we find ourselves in the wilderness. We may not find the types of friends that Dorothy found along the way, but if we search, we can find others to help us. We may not find the same kinds of dangers along the way that Dorothy found, but we will find dangers, including Wolves with big teeth, ready to devour us. Spiders, black and shiny, spinning webs to trap us. And Owllike Creatures, screeching as they fly down from the heavens, salivating, as they seek to capture our souls with their razor-sharp talons. And we may find black skies with no sun, moon, or stars. We may find hollowed-out people. And we may find Dark Ones dressed in fancy robes who spew lies and hatred our way.

Sometimes we will inhabit our new worlds briefly. Sometimes we will find ourselves living in our new worlds for a very long time. At some point, we may begin to realize that we can't go back to how things were, to how we ordinarily lived our lives. Before. For nothing will ever be exactly as we left it. And all we have left is to fight to move forward. And search for the light.

In *The Wizard of Oz*, Dorothy came home by clicking her sparkling red shoes together. And in the end, she was surprised to know that she could have gone home earlier. If only she had known the power of those shoes.

For us, in the real world, things are not as simple. If only we could just click our heels together and find ourselves back in the world from whence we came! Living out our lives as we ordinarily lived out our lives.

But it is not so simple. And we too, like God's people of long ago, have to build houses in our new worlds, plant gardens, marry, have children, and live in peace. We have to move forward in the best way we can. And sometimes we have to wait for a very long time before God takes us to the place he has prepared for us.

And sometimes there is much suffering while we wait. Before the Day comes. Before the sun rises once more. Before the Darkness is scattered. Before anything comes. Before everything comes.

"Sometimes we have to wait for a very long time."
Attribution: Marjatta

PART I

The In-Between Time

Life between Darkness and Light

Satan himself masquerades as an angel of light. It is not surprising,

then, if his servants masquerade as servants of righteousness.

—2 Corinthians 11:14b–15a (NIV)

CHAPTER 1

The Dark Ones are adept at hiding who they really are. They may hide unseen in our homes. They may hide in our places of work, behind smiling faces and false words. They may hide in our children's schools, behind teachers' desks. They may also hide in our public parks, sitting on benches while they wait for their prey to appear. And they may give speeches in our government buildings or flourish behind sacred words in church pulpits. They present themselves as light, but they are Counterfeit Light, and they all wait for orders from their leader, the Prince of Darkness. The Prince of Darkness wants to destroy. The Prince of Darkness wants our souls.

—*Ordinarily Sarah*

THE UNCERTAINTY AND fear our family experienced during the In-Between Time—our years spent between Darkness and Light—cannot be easily defined. The time was fluid. Unsteady. A moment of light here. A moment of great Darkness there.

And confusion covered everything, seeping in from the top of what was once the pinnacle of our upended world and also from beneath, straight from the corridors of hell. The confusion was like thick syrup that coated our lives, running down our arms, our hands, our fingers, and our legs and feet, which were already sticky and dirty from previous leaks and spills. None of it ever washed off thoroughly enough. Never having enough time to clean up during a moment of light before the next dark spill occurred.

Uncertainty, fear, indecisiveness, insecurity, confusion, self-loathing, blindness: these conditions, along with other equally terrifying ones, are exactly what the Prince of Darkness covets. Each of these is a portal through which Satan can enter into our lives—and Satan, the Prince of Darkness, is relentless.

> During the Time In-Between Darkness and Light
> One may think the worst of the Darkness is done,
> And that light is right around the corner.
> But it is not always so.
> Promises are often broken,
> And assurances may not work out.
> Good intensions are forgotten,

And hope may begin to fade.
Friends may disappear,
Wanting to get on with their own lives,
And family may not want to talk about it anymore,
Leaving much unsaid
And tears unshed.
Hope grows ever dimmer,
And one feels helpless,
Angry,
Even angry with God—
And angry at so many others who promised,
Or assured,
Or forgot,
Or just left
And did nothing.
It is a difficult time,
Watching the Darkness get darker,
And the Light disappear.
Many of us have experienced an In-Between Time.
Many of us want to forget
What
Happencd
Both during and before
This time.
Eventually,
Most of us
Move on from this In-Between Time.
But the disappointment never leaves us.
The sadness stays deep inside,
And the anger journeys even deeper.

This Time of Living Between Darkness and Light
Is a perfect time
For the Dark Ones to invade,
Enabling the Prince of Darkness
to destroy.

The disappointment never leaves us.
The sadness stays deep inside.
(Marjatta)

The In-Between Time of my life lasted for many years. My story is not unlike that of many others who have experienced this period of purgatory. It is a time of being stuck in the middle, not able to move either backward or forward. Some don't survive it. Others think they have survived it … until they discover they have not survived it at all, and Darkness continues to consume them. Most go on with their lives anyway— disillusioned, sad, but determined. Many of these go on to do great things despite the Darkness.

> The In-Between Time, for me,
> Was a time of sitting in Darkness
> and a time of searching for light.
> It was a time of giving up,
> of burying what remained,
> and a time of looking past all the graves.
> It was a time of leaving old dreams
> and a time of creating new ones.
> It was a time of questioning old truths
> and accepting new ones.
> It was a time of dying
> and a time of finding new life.
> It was a time to look deep inside,
> and at the same time,
> it was a time of looking closer at all things outside.
> It was a time to cry
> and a time to laugh out loud.
> It was a time to be angry at God
> and a time to run toward him.

It was a terrible time,
a lonely time,
and a time when joy came lightly.
It was a time of pushing others aside
and a time of growing closer to those standing near.
It was a time to pray
and a time to walk away.
It was a time of no hope at all
and a time for new hope to be discovered.
The In-Between Time was a time when nothing
    mattered,
and a time when everything mattered.

The In-Between Time of my life occupied the ten-year period from the time a judge ruled that we could not take a lawsuit for grandparent visitation rights any further, to the time our daughter, Annie, with her husband and their five children, came out of captivity, and we all entered into the Time After.

Our lengthy legal battle for our Annie and her children had begun in what I call the Time Before, a period that also spanned ten years. By the end of that first decade, our petition for grandparents' rights had been denied. We would not be allowed to see our grandkids. We were defeated, crushed, and hopeless. There were no winners standing before the judge that day. None at all. We had all lost.

Except for the Dark One.

Altogether, it was twenty years from the time our daughter and her family entered captivity until the time they all walked out. During those twenty years, my family and I were plagued with Dark Ones. For many of those years, we were totally unaware of them. We had no clue that the Dark Ones were entrenched in our lives. We did not understand what was not yet understandable. And along with all the not knowing, there was constant pain that sliced through our bodies and our souls. Every single day.

> *There was given to me a thorn in my flesh, a messenger of Satan, to torment me. Three times I pleaded with the Lord to take it away from me. But he said to me, "My grace is sufficient for you, my power is made perfect in weakness."*
> *(2 Corinthians 12:7b–9a NIV)*

The In-Between Time was long and difficult—as painful, if not more painful, than the Time Before.

In the beginning of the Time Before, we still had hope, however small. We believed that we would surely find someone to help us. Perhaps the police, the Department of Family Services, the detectives we hired, or the lawyers eating away at our savings. Surely those who had defected from the group would help us? Our Christian counselor. The judge, perhaps? Or surely God would!

But after the court hearing, as the Time Before ended and the In-Between Time began, hope nearly vanished. No one had been able to help us. Not even God.

At the very beginning of our twenty-year journey, we had not known or understood the extent of our plight. It had all begun quite innocently. And it had happened slowly, gradually. We had no idea what was really happening to us. We later learned that we had been like lambs led to the slaughter.

Somewhere, in the beginning of that first ten-year span, a Dark One (a Wolf disguised as a lamb, or, in our case, a Wolf disguised as a beautiful woman dressed in fancy robes) entered our lives. We did not know her very well, but she seemed nice enough, so we let her in. We were totally unaware of who she really was.

Then, one day, she simply blew our lives to pieces. She took everything from us. And she managed to claw out parts of our hearts and minds, injuring all of us … permanently.

We had been such fools! We had built our lives with straw and sticks, believing that nothing untoward could happen to us. After all, we were Christians. My husband and I were pastors of a thriving congregation. All our children had been baptized. They had all attended Sunday school. They were all confirmed in the faith. They participated in high school church activities. We were all active in our community. We were *good people*. Nothing remotely dark could possibly enter our lives.

But the Wolf, disguised as a beautiful lady dressed in fancy robes, had walked right into our lives and shattered us. Totally blindsiding us! This Dark One had decided she wanted our souls. She would do anything to get them, and she nearly destroyed us. We have carried the pain of broken souls ever since.

There was given me a thorn in my flesh, a messenger of Satan. (2 Corinthians 12:7b NIV)

Had we only known at the end of that first ten-year span that our daughter and her family would all escape from their captivity and come home one day, the world might not have felt so broken. Our souls would not have felt so crushed. But there was no knowing. Suffering seemed unending. Darkness turned ever darker, and Day was nowhere to be found. It seemed to be the end of everything after the judge told us no. It was the beginning of the In-Between Time as we gathered ourselves together and decided we had to move on. The worst had happened. It was over. We were not going to see our daughter or our grandchildren again—perhaps not ever. It was over. Done. Finished.

Where is Day?
Where are all the people?
Where are all the calling birds?
Only Darkness is here
and cold winds blowing
and hollowed-out souls crying out for help.
Where is morning?
Where is noon?

Where is any time at all?
Only night remains,
and time stands still,
and nothing moves upon the earth.
Where is Day hidden?
Must we seek her hiding place alone?
Must we push away the Darkness on our own?
Will no one help us?
Will not Day come soon?
Where is Day's Light?
Where is Day?
—*Ordinarily Sarah*

CHAPTER 2

FOR ME, THE dark In-Between Time was mostly a time of trying to put the past behind us and willing myself to move forward. Most importantly, it was a time for me to figure out how to survive. I knew, if I chose to do so, I could simply give up and succumb to the Darkness. Others do. But that would have been far too easy. I did not really want to go there.

I chose, instead, to push through it. Hope or no hope, I chose to push through it. And every dark day, I pushed and pushed. I labored. I sweated. I screamed inside. I cried, inside, so no one could see my tears. And with every dark day that arrived, I hoped—and it was seemingly my only hope—I would make it to the other side this time. To where Day lived. To where Darkness turned to Light. Every single day was a battle! And every single day, I felt the pain of the thorn in my side.

Besides putting the past behind, the In-Between Time was also a time for me to question everything. Who was I? What was important for my life? What wasn't? Who was important in my life? Everyone? No one? What was real? What was not real? What was truth? What was not truth? Should I search for truth? Or was truth right before me? Should I hide from truth? Or was I already hiding from the truth? Where was God? And how could God have let this happen to us? And sometimes I would give in for a while and simply sit in the Darkness, and not question anything at all. Not think about anything at all.

But thinking of nothing at all never lasted long. Old questions always resurfaced. And new questions surfaced with the old ones. How was I to survive when part of my family had vanished? Would I ever see my daughter again? How in the world could this have happened? And where was God?

If only I had known that they would all come out one day, on their own.

But I did not know. None of us knew. God knew, but God wasn't telling us anything. Anything at all. God was nowhere to be found.

We had to move ahead,
in brokenness,
and in overwhelming sorrow.
And wait for a time
when the world would be up-righted once more.
For a time when Daylight would come.
For a time when God would scatter the Darkness.

There is a time for everything,

And a season for every activity under heaven:
A time to be born and a time to die,
A time to plant and a time to uproot,
A time to kill and a time to heal,
A time to tear down and a time to build,
A time to weep and a time to laugh,
A time to mourn and a time to dance,
A time to scatter stones and a time to gather
them,
A time to embrace and a time to refrain,
A time to search and a time to give up,
A time to keep and a time to throw away,
A time to tear and a time to mend,
A time to be silent and a time to speak,
A time to love and a time to hate,
A time for war and a time for peace.
—Ecclesiastes 3:1–8 (NIV)

But during the In-Between Time, I was often unable to figure out a time for anything at all. It was difficult to find direction. And the Darkness that continued to invade my life was unforgiving. In my mind's eye, my life lay before me in one jumbled mess, thrown together in no particular pattern or purpose. It was like a large pile of discarded thread found at the back of a dusty attic, all bunched up and stuffed into an oversized plastic bag, bursting over with the twisted threads of various colors and lengths and thicknesses. And knots. With seemingly no beginning. And no ending. And no way to unravel any of it. No way of sorting it all out.

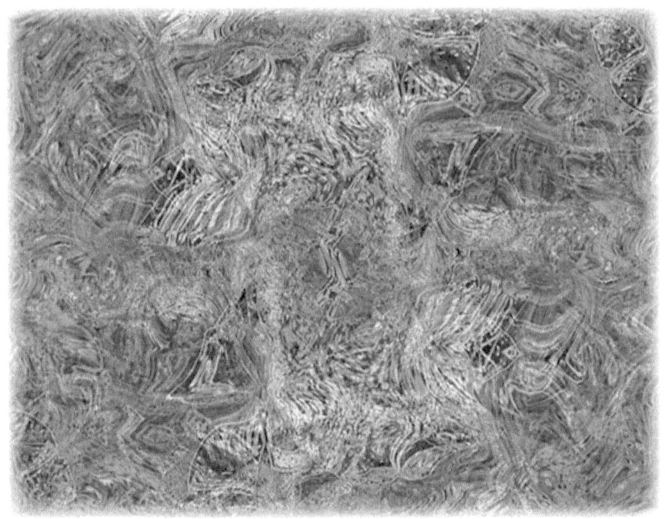

My life lay before me in one
jumbled-up mess, thrown
together in no particular pattern or purpose.
Kris Stoyer, graphic artist

If only I could have actually seen the mass of thread *outside* of my mind's eye, perhaps I could have dealt with it. Picked it up from a real floor of a real attic. Thrown it away. Burned it. I could have begun my life in a new direction. Changed it. Made it right. But I could see it only in my mind's eye.

And I often asked where God was. Could someone tell me, please. Where was God hiding? I could not see God in my mind's eye. I could not see God hovering over the mass of twisted thread that was my life. Surely God could fix this! But no one could tell me where God was. And no one could convince me God was near. And every time I thought about God's absence, the thorn tore at my flesh even more, telling me to forget about God. That thinking about God only brought pain.

> *For the Lord is a great God,*
> *and a great King above all gods.*
> *In his hand are the depths of the earth,*
> *the heights of the mountains are his also.*
> *The sea is his for he made it,*
> *and his hands formed the dry land.*
> *Oh come, let us worship and bow down,*
> *let us kneel before the Lord our Maker;*
> *For he is our God*
> *and we are the people of his pasture,*
> *and the sheep of his hand.*
> *—Psalm 95:3–7 (ESV)*

But I could not find him! I could not find him! Why could I not find God?

And in time, I gave up looking for God hovering over the mass of twisted thread that was my life. And about the same time, I discovered that there was more than just a big plastic bag full of tangled thread that I saw inside my mind. There was something else. Something dark and dangerous! Somewhere inside that mass of tangled thread, something untoward had settled in. And I discovered a spider web—with a Spider in it! The Spider met my gaze and stared at me with bright eyes. And it told me it was waiting for me to falter. Waiting for me to give up. Waiting for just the right time. To trap my soul. And completely destroy it.

Where are you, God? I can't find you! My life is a tangled-up mess. The Wolf deceived me. The thorn hurts! And the Spider frightens me! Help me, God!

I could see the Spider spinning. I could feel its heart throbbing as it worked. I felt it throbbing right along with my own heartbeat. Only faster. And more urgently. Making its web bigger. Stickier. Thicker. Darker. Steadily spinning. Ever spinning. If only I could have swept it away.

But I could not. It was deep inside my mind's eye. In the midst of all of the tangled threads.

And I thought to myself, *If only I could find the main thread I needed from inside the tangled-up mess.* If I pulled it, I believed it might untangle the entire mess and allow me to sweep away the Spider and its web along with all the thread. But it was all out of my reach. Tucked safely inside of my mind's eye.

I would not be able to find the particular thread I needed.

And I wondered if that main thread might actually be woven into the web itself. And if so, were other threads woven into the web as well? Was it possible that some of the threads were so tightly woven into that spider trap that their beginnings and endings were indistinguishable from the web? Were all the threads, and the web, woven together into one huge clump of confusion and disarray? And Darkness?

Impossible to destroy? Would this be my life forever after? How would I survive? How would I ever be able to move forward, all tangled up? And trapped by a Spider that wanted to destroy my soul?

The Spider met my gaze and stared
at me with piercing, bright eyes.
Kris Stoyer, graphic artist

One thing I promised myself during the In Between Time was that hope or no hope, thorn or no thorn, I would not allow the tangled-up mass of thread with its ugly web and Spider to permanently hold me back. I wouldn't allow it to paralyze my soul with fear forever.

I knew I had to push on. I had to find a way to survive! I told myself that I would eventually find a way to unravel the jumbled mass, expose the web inside, sweep the Spider away, and find the Light. I would eventually find the main thread, and that would reveal everything with one pull. The thread that would clearly expose the shiny, dark tenant with its strong, hairy legs, ever working, ever spinning. And ever trying to destroy me.

I wished I could understand what it all meant, but nothing was yet understandable to me.

And most days, I was too tired to do anything at all, let alone push forward. I was too tired to think about anything. Too tired to move at all. Any little bit of energy I did have had to be used for one thing: survival. And I became relentless in my desire to survive.

On many days, all I could do was utter a small prayer I had learned in my childhood:

> Now I lay me down to sleep
> I pray thee lord my soul to keep
> And if I die before I wake,
> I pray thee lord my soul to take.
> —Twentieth-century prayer attributed to
> Joseph Addison

Where are you hiding, God? I cannot find you! Are you perhaps inside that tangled-up mass within me? But, no, you can't be there. There is no light in that place. And you are Light.

And every day that went by,
Every dark day,
I grew wearier,
and I felt more alone.
And I longed to be comforted,
but there was no comfort at all.
Where was Day?
Would not Day come soon?
Would not Day peek around the hills?
Scatter the Darkness,
And bring comfort and warmth?
Where was Day?
Where was God?

Comfort, comfort my people, says your God. Speak tenderly to Jerusalem. A voice cries: "In the wilderness prepare the way of the Lord; make straight in the desert a highway for our God. Every valley shall be lifted up, and every mountain and hill be made low; the uneven ground shall become level, and the rough places a plain. And the glory of the Lord shall be revealed, and all flesh shall see it together, for the mouth of the Lord has spoken." He gives power to the faint, and to him who has no might he increases strength. ... but they who wait for the Lord shall renew their strength; they shall mount up with wings like eagles; they shall run and not be weary; they shall walk and not faint. (Isaiah 40:1–2a, 3–5, 29, 31 ESV)

But most days, my hope was weak, fragile. And the Spider kept weaving. And watching. And spinning. Waiting for me to falter and to fall. And I did not know how to make the Spider stop. I did not know how to make the crooked roads straight. I did not know how to make the rough places smooth. I did not know how to untangle the threads. My strength was no more. I could not soar like an eagle. The pain in my flesh was overwhelming. I could not see the Lord. I could not comfort any people. I could find no comfort for myself. And I felt I was forever lost in the night. Waiting for the Light that was Day. Waiting for someone to come. Waiting for God.

> Lost in the night do the people yet languish,
> Longing for morning the Darkness to vanquish,
> Plaintively heaving a sigh full of anguish,
> Will not day come soon? Will not day come soon?
> —Lost in The Night," an old Finnish folk tune

Would God ever come? Would the nightmare ever be over? Would the sun ever rise? Would the Spider ever stop its spinning? Would the Darkness ever scatter? Would my daughter ever come home? Would help ever come? Would the waiting ever be over? Would my life ever be ordinary again? Would the thorn ever stop hurting?

The Pretty Lady in Fancy Robes took away everything.

She took away my child,
She took away my grandchild.
She took away my five grandchildren yet to come.
She took away my work,
She took away my purpose for life.
She took away joy,
She took away tears.
She took away sleep at night,
And she took away peace at daybreak.
She took away my family,
And she took away my family-to-be.
She took away memories.
She took away the present,
And she took away my dreams for a future.
She took away color and light.
She took away laughter.
She took away pieces of my heart,
And slices of my soul.
She took away the world as I once knew it,
And she took away my courage to rebuild it.
Most terrible of all,
She almost took away my faith.
And she nearly,
Took away God.
—*Ordinarily Sarah*

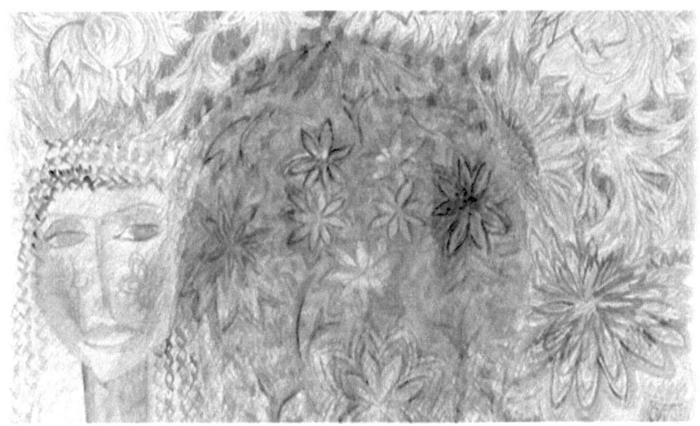

The Pretty Lady in Fancy Robes took away
everything—and she kept it in a jar.
Marjatta

*Where are you, God? Where are you hiding? Won't you
please pull this thorn from my flesh?*

But it was a long, long wait before any of my
questions about my life—or about anything at all—
would be answered. Looking back, I believe it was a
good thing that I did not know how lengthy the wait
would be before my questions would be answered. I
could not have stood it.

I decided that perhaps it was a good thing that
the pain of the thorn in my flesh was constant. The
pain reminded me, every single day, that I had to
keep pushing. I could not give up. I could not quit.
If I wanted to be free of the pain, I could not give
up—until it was done.

If only I had understood. But I could not
understand what was not yet understandable to me.

CHAPTER 3

AND IT WAS years later, long after the Time Before, when the Sky Turned Black and the Owls came for my daughter. Long after the legal battle began and ended. Long after the In-Between Time had begun. And long after many dark days, weeks, months, and years of pushing myself to survive and move forward, that I came to understand what I wanted to happen, and when I wanted it to happen, was not for me to decide. I had absolutely no control over time or over anything else!

I had no control over when the Spider and its web would be swept away. I had no control over the tangled-up mess that was my life. I had no control over the one thread I wanted found. I had no control over the unraveling of all the other threads. It was not up to me to determine the time for my daughter and her family to come home. It was not my call to be set free of the Darkness. It was not my call to have the painful thorn in my flesh removed. And it was not my call when the time would come to find the

Light. Not yet. I had no control over anything. My time and my way were not God's time or God's way. God's time and God's way were God's alone.

I had to wait. Until God was ready. Until I could understand what was not yet understandable. Until I could fully understand that in the beginning when the Sky Turned Black, and then later, when the judge told us "No," God's plan was working its way out. God's plan had to come first: the In-Between Time, and the tangled-up thread, and the Spider and its web. It all had to come first. It was all part of God's plan. And, yes, suffering was a part of that plan. The suffering had to come first. Before anything else could come. Before I could understand anything. Anything at all.

I had to fully understand that what we had to endure was important.

It all had to come before anything else could come. Before the main thread could be discovered and pulled to unravel all the other threads. Before the Spider and its web could be found and destroyed. Before my daughter could come home. Before the truth could arrive. Before the Light that was Day could peek around the mountains. Before the Darkness could be scattered. Before the pain of the thorn could be lessened. All of it had to come first.

Before all the rest.
Before I could see the morning star,
Before all things were made new,
Before our daughter came home,

Before the sun rose once more,
Before the fullness of day came,
Before the Darkness was scattered,
Before the Lord came to save us,
Before anything,
Before everything!

I needed to understand that all that was happening or had already happened was much bigger and darker than anything or anyone could have known. Much bigger and darker than anything the judge could have known. Or the lawyers. Or the police. Or anyone else. Or anything anyone could have known.

For what none of us had known at that court hearing, and what none of us had known during the ten years before that, was that dozens of Spiders had quietly begun to settle into our lives, and into the lives of many of the people around us. And the Spiders were weaving webs of confusion, deceit, and Darkness inside all of us. The Spiders were Dark Ones. And no one knew it. No one had understood.

The Spiders were Dark Ones. And no one
knew. No one had understood.
Kris Stoyer

And no one in my family had known that the Lady
in Fancy Robes who had entered our lives was also
a Dark One, a Wolf. And the Spiders, the Owls,
the nightmares, the daymares, the Dragon, even the
Darkness that had invaded our lives, were all also
Dark Ones, all sent by the Evil One. The Prince of
Darkness. All sent to us to destroy our souls. None
of us had known that our souls were about to be
devoured. We had not known any of it. We had not
understood evil.

And the thread I had thought was so important was not a thread at all. There was no such thread that could unravel the mess. There was only God. God was the only one able to unravel it all, defeat the enemy, and reveal the pathway to the Light. To Day. I had not understood. None of us had understood. I had believed that evil would never come to our house, come into our lives. Evil went to other people's houses, to other, less godly people's houses.

But I was wrong.

In the beginning, I had not fully understood the vision I had of that Legion of Destroyers swooping down from the heavens to snatch away my daughter's soul. I had thought it was just a nightmare.

But I was wrong. It had been more.

That vision had come to me the same day our daughter called to say that her relationship with us—and with everyone else in the family—was over. Done! Perhaps forever! The vision I had of the Legion of Destroyers coming down from heaven was real. The Day the Sky Turned Black and the sun and moon fell down was real. The Wolf, the Fancy Lady, the tangled threads, the Spider and its web, the nightmares, the daymares, it was all real. And it was all connected. Connected to my daughter's disappearance. Connected to my husband and me. Connected to our ministry.

My daughter, her husband, and their only child vanished that Day the Sky Turned Black. Their souls had crumbled like dead moths in the talons of the Owls. Their bodies were left hollow, torn apart, lifeless. Their eyes, plucked out, were left unseeing. Their mouths were left forever in the shape of screams. It was all real.

And we had not understood any of it. Because we had not yet understood evil. We had not yet understood that evil had come to our home. And we had not fought what we had not understood.

I thought it had all been just a dream.

But I had been wrong!

And every dark day, during the absence of my daughter and her family, I had felt compelled to pray, without fully understanding why:

Now I lay *them* down to sleep,
I pray Thee Lord *their* souls to keep.
And if *they* die before they wake,
I pray Thee Lord *their* souls to take.
(adapted from Joseph Addison's "Now I Lay Me
    Down to Sleep.")
I prayed, without fully understanding.
But God did.
God understood.
God understood everything.
And God had a plan.
For hope.
And for a future.
For us.

Where was Light? Would Day ever come? I asked these questions over and over again, but I had not understood that Day could come only by God's hand and only in God's time. There was no other way. I had not fully understood it. I had thought I could fix it all by myself. I had not understood that I was too heavy with the Darkness that came from the enemy. I was too sluggish and weak and ill-informed to do anything at all. To understand anything at all.

I had to fully understand God's power. And I had to fully understand that only God could scatter the Darkness. No one else! No policemen. No lawyers. No detectives. No law. No judge. No court. No anybody. No one else. Least of all me.

And so it was, in the beginning, I had not understood much of anything. I had not understood much of anything for a long, long time. Past the Time Before. And past most of the In-Between Time. And in my lack of understanding, my anger at God took over. And my bitterness. Where was God? I did not understand. I did not know if I would ever understand. Where was God?

> *Today also my complaint is bitter; my hand*
> *is heavy on account of my groaning. Oh that*
> *I knew where I might find him, that I might*
> *come even to his seat! I would lay my case*
> *before him and fill my mouth with arguments.*
> *I would know what he would answer me and*
> *understand what he would say to me. Would he*
> *contend with me in the greatness of his power?*
> *No; he would pay attention to me. There an*

upright man could argue with him, and I would be acquitted forever by my judge. Behold I go forward, but he is not there; and backward, but I do not perceive him; on the left hand when he is working, I do not behold him; he turns to the right hand, but I do not see him. ... God has made my heart faint; the Almighty has terrified me; yet I am not silenced because of the Darkness, nor because thick Darkness covers my face. (Job 23:2–9, 16–17 ESV)

Where was God? Where was anybody? The people who could have helped had failed. Our state's Department of Children and Family Services had failed. Our local police departments had failed. Our lawyers had failed. Our private detectives had failed. The judge had failed. The justice system had failed. I had failed. God had failed! Where was God? I had not fully understood anything. Anything at all.

Why then did you bring me out of the womb?
I wished I had died before any eye saw me.
If only I had never come into being,
Or had been carried straight from to the womb
to the grave.
Are not my few days almost over?
Turn away from me so I can have a moment's joy
Before I go to the place of no return,
To the land of gloom and deep shadow.

To the land of deepest night,
Of deep shadow and disorder,
Where even light is like darkness.
(Job 10:18–22 NIV)

And so it was, as the In-Between Time wore on, I made the decision to distance myself from everything that had happened. I needed to escape from the Darkness. I needed to forget about it all. I decided I would think no more about the court hearing—or any of the events leading up to it. Or about any of the events that had happened since. I would make myself feel nothing. I would not say anything about any of it. I would, as best as I could, not think about any of it.

I would simply push on, making myself become as I once had been, before the sun and moon dropped out of the sky and the Owls with sharp talons invaded our daughter's life. Before the dragon came. Before the nightmares. Before the visions. Before the dreams. Before our daughter and her family vanished. Before the Wolf blew our lives apart. And before the Spiders began their spinning. I would make myself be as I once had been: Ordinarily Sarah. Plain, unsuspecting Sarah. Ordinarily living out her ordinary life

I would lock it all up. Shut it all away. I would make myself believe that nothing important had occurred. I would make myself believe that it had all been a bad dream. I had no daughter. I had no grandchildren. I had made it all up.

What I didn't know at the time was that by making

that decision, I was letting evil win. At least for a time. But I did not understand. I did not understand what was not yet understandable. I did not understand that all of it had to come first. Before the rest could come. I understood nothing. And so I was stuck in the In-Between Time for a very long while.

But, somehow, I still survived.

CHAPTER 4

I THOUGHT I KNEW what I had to do in order to survive—clear out my thoughts, start over, and get rid of the Darkness—but I wasn't sure how to accomplish it all. And as time passed, I decided that it was all too difficult. I had to have help. Alone, I would not be able to keep a lid on all I had experienced. The Darkness was too heavy. Too vast. Too complicated. And since I could not find God, I decided I needed to find someone else to help me.

What I had not understood was the thinking that I, Sarah, had some power over the Darkness. I still thought that I, or some other person I knew, could fix it all. In reality, by thinking that, I was letting evil win.

And so, clueless, and faced with the fact that I did not know where to go for help, I continued to struggle. At the same time, I sensed that all who knew me thought I was doing okay. Thought I was moving on with my life. What they did not know was that I was good at pretending.

I had to find someone I could trust and confide in. But at the same time, I sensed that most people who knew my situation just wanted me to stop talking about it and move on.

Even those who had firsthand information about the church my daughter was involved in wanted me to stop talking about it.

Truth was, many of us, particularly those who had children and grandchildren inside of that strange church, were battling demons. Were battling Darkness. Were battling with a lack of understanding as to what the battle was really all about! And most of these people believed that God had seemingly disappeared from their lives.

I did not know what to do in order to move forward. I was on my own. And the Darkness was unending. The Spiders were spinning day and night. And none of us had a clue as to what was really going on.

> Hey diddle, diddle
> The cat and the fiddle
> The cow jumped over the moon.
> The little dog never saw such a sight in his life,
> And the dish ran away with the spoon.
> —A child's nursery rhyme

My world had tilted. And just like in the nursery rhyme, in my world, a cat was fiddling. A cow was jumping over the moon. And a dish was running away with a spoon. When would my world be turned upright again? When would the sun peek out from around the mountains? When would the Darkness scatter? When would I wake up from this nightmare? And where in the world was God?

In time, I decided the only choice I had was to open up some of the little compartments inside my mind that I had so carefully built to store my worst thoughts and memories. My worst daymares and nightmares. Maybe there were some answers in those little compartments. For sure, I was not getting any answers from anywhere else. Had I mistakenly put away thoughts and ideas and memories that could be of help to me?

But a part of me did not really want to open up those compartments at all.

For some time, I had been banishing away thought after thought to those little compartments. I had been erasing experience after experience by hiding them inside. I was pushing away everything that hurt when I thought about it.

Why would I want to undo all of my work?

I had even pushed aside several parts of my core self that I believed I no longer needed. Split them off my core with an ax. Took away their voices. Made them sit alone in the dark. These living, breathing parts of me only reminded me of what had been. And I didn't always like what they had to say!

But I felt alone. And weak. And tired. Did I need to take back those other parts of me? Could I use some of their ideas, some of their strengths, some of their wisdom? Did I need their eyes and their ears?

Did I need to be whole again? No longer split apart in pieces? Just because I believed I had no more use for them? Or because I didn't particularly like them? Or because they were annoying to me?

If a house is divided against itself,
that house cannot stand.
—Mark 3:25 (NIV)

But I already knew the answers to many of my questions. I needed to reopen all the little compartments I had so carefully constructed. I needed to call out to the other living, breathing parts of me that I had pushed aside. I needed to ask them to come back home!

And so I did! And just like that, my life began changing and reshaping itself. Every moment different than the last.

And just like Alice in Wonderland, who claimed her life became curiouser and curiouser as she ventured through the looking glass, so too did my life become curiouser and curiouser as I entered a portal to yet another new world.

CHAPTER 5

I T WAS DURING this time of upheaval and change and curious goings-on that I had an amazing revelation from God. It was revealed to me that God was near to me after all! He had been near to me all along! How had I missed him? How? He had not abandoned me after all! He had never abandoned me! He had not disappeared. Despite every angry word I had directed at him. Despite every fearful thought I had conjured up concerning his existence. Despite every action of rebellion. God had never left me!

> *My God! My God! Why*
> *have you forsaken me?*
> *—Matthew 27:46 (ESV)*

I had been stuck there in that same place where Jesus had been stuck while he hung on his cross. Stuck in that place of wondering, of questioning, of perhaps even doubting. Only Jesus was stuck for only a moment. I had been stuck in that place for a long,

long time. That place of wondering whether God was with me or not.

Had I forgotten what Jesus had said right after?

For right after calling out, "My God, my God! Why have you forsaken me?" from Matthew 27:46 (ESV), in Luke 23:46, Jesus called out "Father, into your hands I commit my spirit."

Jesus knew his Father had not forsaken him. And Jesus committed his spirit into his Father's hands. These were Jesus's last words from his cross: "Father, into your hands I commit my spirit."

And after that one short moment of wondering, of perhaps questioning why he had to suffer alone, of perhaps questioning why he had to suffer at all, of perhaps questioning his Father's plans, or perhaps of questioning his Father's very existence, Jesus finally understood fully. He finally fully understood why he had to suffer—and suffer alone. He finally fully understood God's plan. He finally fully understood that his Father had not forsaken him at all! His Father was near to him. Jesus was not alone. The feeling of being alone was simply a part of the suffering that Jesus had to endure. It was a part of God's plan. And Jesus—finally and fully understanding his Father's purpose and plan for him—committed his spirit into his Father's hands.

And what had taken Jesus only a moment to fully understand, had taken me more than a decade. And it was toward the end of that decade that I had become angrier and angrier at God.

When I look back to those weeks a short time ago, I realize I just had not understood. I had not understood anything! And I had been absolutely furious with God! I had even decided that since God had been so absent in my life, I did not want to believe in him anymore! *What good was believing in an absent God?*

And in my moments of being furious with God, I had thought that God had abandoned me. I had not understood anything at all.

But it was just a few days after being so furious with God that I began to have second thoughts about my unbelief. And I asked myself how I could not believe in God. If I decided to think that way, I would be betraying my faith. Betraying God. Betraying God's people. Betraying my very life! And all hope would be gone. Forever! All would be Darkness from birth to death. And death would have the final word. Death would bring a Darkness that would last for an eternity. Is that what I wanted to believe?

And a few weeks later, after having had all these thoughts and questions about God, he revealed to me that he *was* near to me after all!

Curiouser and curiouser! One moment I had been questioning God's existence, and the next, God revealed to me that he was near!

The revelation occurred early one evening, at church, in the middle of choir practice! There, in the choir loft, in the middle of the alto section where I sang, it was revealed to me that the biggest crisis in my life was not the losing of my daughter and her family at all! The biggest crisis in my life was that I had thought I did not believe in God anymore! Had I lost my faith?

How long had I been thinking that God might not exist? How long had I been struggling with my faith? Had I been merely pretending to believe? What kind of a pastor was I? How had I descended into such Darkness?

And I cried out, "My Lord and my God! Drive the thorn deeper! I deserve only pain! Forgive me for doubting your existence!"

> *Then [Jesus] said to Thomas, "Put your finger here; see my hands. Reach out your hand and put it into my side. Stop doubting and believe." Thomas said to Jesus, "My Lord and my God!" Then Jesus said to Thomas, "Because you have seen me you have believed; blessed are those who have not seen and yet have believed." (John 20:27–29 NIV)*

And that very night, right in the middle of choir practice, I began to pray quietly. And as I was praying, the choir began to sing more beautifully than I had ever heard before. Our voices began traveling upward, past the ceiling, past the night sky, past all the stars, and finally into the heavenly realms, where our voices joined a choir of angels.

And as we continued to sing with the angels, I

begged God to help me believe! I cried out to God to banish my unbelief! I begged God to help me give it all up: the pain, the sorrow, the hurt, the anger! I asked God to restore my faith! I asked God to forgive me! "I repent, Lord! I repent of my unbelief! Forgive me and help me believe!"

And at once, a veil dropped from my eyes. And I understood. All of it. I understood what at first had not been understandable to me. I understood that I had to let go of the world I had yoked myself to and yoke myself instead to Christ alone. I understood that in order to yoke myself to Christ, I had to endure suffering.

And the suffering had to come first. Before anything else.

I repented of my unbelief. I asked God for forgiveness. I confessed that I had not trusted in him and that, instead, I had been trying to do things on my own. I confessed that I had been hiding away things I did not like in the back rooms and on the top shelves of my mind. Because I had been afraid. And angry. And rebellious. And I had not trusted. And I had not understood. I had not understood anything at all!

But suddenly I understood everything! First, the suffering had to come. Then the grief. Then the anger. Then the unbelief. Then the discovery that God was near! Then repentance. Then forgiveness. And then, finally, the full understanding! The understanding of what had not been understandable to me before. It all had to come before any of the rest could come.

Before Day could finally come.

I had failed as a pastor and as a human being. I had nearly lost my faith in God. I had not wanted God in my life anymore. I had kept some of what God had provided for me hidden in little compartments on high dusty shelves in the back rooms of my mind. Easy to ignore. Easy to forget. Thinking I knew better. Thinking I was smarter than God. Thinking I was in control of my life. And in control of everything else that mattered to me.

I had even pushed away living, breathing pieces of me! I had taken an ax and cut them off. And they now lay splintered, as small pieces of unusable wood, kindling wood, useless, unless set on fire! What had I done?

I had come to the end of me. And it had to come to pass before I could understand what had not been understandable to me for a long, long time. Before I could know that God had been with me all along. Before I could know that God alone was the one who could unravel all the threads. Not some magic thread! Before I could know that it was God alone who could destroy the Spider and its web. Nothing else. No one else. It was God alone who could chase away the Wolf, the Owllike Creatures, the Darkness, the daymares, and the nightmares.

And I had done my very best to banish God from my life! I had given in to the Darkness. I had given in to the Dark Ones. In the beginning, I had even given in to the Owllike Creatures with their long, sharp talons, screeching as they flew down from the heavens to devour their prey. I had given in by pretending that none of it was true. It wasn't true when the Sky Turned Black and the world fell on its side. It wasn't true that a phone call came from my daughter, telling me she could not see me anymore. Evil did not exist. None of it was true. It had all been just a nightmare.

How had I given in to it all?

By not believing it could happen.

By not believing that evil was in the world. By not believing that evil, if it did exist, would ever harm me or my family!

And after all of the pretending ended, the long legal battle began. I could not pretend anymore. And eventually, the end of everything came. In a courtroom. From words spoken by a judge. And the beginning of the In-Between Time came. And I came to the end of me.

All of this had to come before I could understand what had not yet been understandable.

God had been with me from the very beginning,
when the Prince of Darkness had begun stalking
my family,
as a Wolf in sheep's clothing,
(or as a Pretty Lady in Fancy Robes).
God had been with me when my daughter called
to tell me she couldn't see me anymore.
God had been with me when my daughter and her
family vanished.
When their souls had crumbled like dead moths,

And their bodies were left hollow,
with unseeing eyes,
and mouths closed shut.
God had been with me when I could no longer cry.
God himself had cried for me, in my place.
God had been with me when I had made myself
    blind
to the Dark Ones.
God had been with me when my husband told me
he had had a glimmer of something untoward
forming in our lives.
And I wouldn't believe him.
God had even been with me when I decided
to cut away living, breathing parts of me
with an ax!

But I was the one who had made my own tangled-up
mass of thread. I was the one who let the Pretty Lady
with Fancy Robes blow our lives apart! I was the one
who allowed the Spiders to spin. I was the one who
hid things I did not like in the back of my mind, and
I was the one who hacked off living, breathing parts
of me, with an ax. And so I cried out:

Forgive me, Lord! The end of me has come.
Restore in me a clean spirit.
Make me whole again!
I need all the parts of me to survive.
All that you created of me.

I cannot survive as a trunk without leaves and branches.

And I cannot survive without you!

Lord God, lift up the living, breathing pieces of me from the kindling pile, dry and useless. Restore their voices. Set them free. Bring them back to me. I need them! And I need all the other compartments opened up and laid bare. I need to see what is hidden in them!

Most of all, I need you!

And, Lord, forgive me for thinking I was ever in control of anything. I had no right to hide things. To take up the ax. To cut off the branches from the trunk. You are the true Gardener, God. Not me. Did I think I had more authority than you?

You, God, are in charge. Of everything! Not me.

I am the true vine, and my Father is the gardener. He cuts off every branch in me that bears no fruit, while every branch that does bear fruit he prunes. Remain in me and I will remain in you. No branch can bear fruit by itself; it must remain in the vine. Neither can you bear fruit unless you remain in me. I am the vine; you are the branches. If a person remains in me and I in him, he will bear much fruit. Apart from me you can do nothing. If anyone

*does not remain in me, he is like a branch that
is thrown away and withers; such branches are
picked up, thrown into the fire and burned. If
you remain in me and my words remain in you,
ask whatever you wish, and it will be given to
you. (John 15:1–7 NIV)*

I had gotten everything wrong:

> I had thought I could control my own life.
> I had denied the existence of the Evil One.
> I did not want to believe that something
> Terrible and powerful
> Existed in my world.

For years, I had chosen to do things my own way. I had worked with many different people to get my daughter and her family out of the abusive religious group she belonged to. Lawyers. Private detectives. The police. Family Social Services. Ex-group members. I had chosen to do everything in my power to get my daughter and her family out of that group. I had not trusted God. I had not thought God was smart enough. Fast enough.

And I had built those small compartments in my mind to fill with thoughts, ideas, and experiences I had not wanted to deal with. Instead of praying to God for help. I had even cut off pieces of me with an ax because I had decided I had no more need of them. Instead of honoring what God had made!

I had closed my eyes to God when I thought he was moving too slowly. And I had decided that I could do it all on my own.

Better.
Faster.
But I was so wrong.
Deadly wrong.
And I came to the end of me.
I had not trusted in God.
And I came to the end of me.
And it was then that I asked God for mercy.
And he gave me mercy.
I asked God to forgive me.
And he gave me forgiveness.
I asked God to make me whole again.
And he made me whole.
All the king's horses and all the king's men,
Couldn't put me together again.
But God could.
And God did!

CHAPTER 6

CURIOUSER AND CURIOUSER. Alice would have been amazed. For all at once, one of the branches that I had severed from my core self stood strong and tall and confident before me.

I had let her help me in the beginning. She had helped me put locks on many of my thoughts. She had dragged the poisonous thoughts to the back of my mind, to the high and dusty shelves, to where all the little boxes were stored. She had been afraid that the dark thoughts would destroy me. She had helped me sort out all my thoughts. She had believed that by locking up all the hurtful thoughts, dreams, and experiences in the little boxes, I would be able to focus on ordinary things. Everyday things. Normal things. So that my core self could move forward. And survive. She believed she was protecting my core self by helping to hide what she believed I did not want or need in my life!

But she didn't always ask for my permission before she hid things from me. And I grew more and more unhappy with her. I grew tired of her domineering ways. And I had taken the ax and cut her off from me.

This living, breathing part of me I had cut off! I had not liked the fact that she had locked away so many of my thoughts without asking me! Troubling thoughts about nightmares. Thoughts I had about disturbing visions, feelings of inadequacy, confusion, fear, and other things. I believed that I had the right to have the final say about whether these things should be remembered. Or not.

This part of me was bold and bossy and loud and was always trying to tell me what was best for me! I didn't want her with me anymore!

And now, here she was, standing before me. She had not been burnt up in a fire. God had saved her. God had pruned her. And now she stood straight and strong before me. And her branches were bearing much fruit.

I had relegated her to a kindling pile. I had silenced her. Now this dying, spindly branch had been rescued from the kindling pile, and she stood straight and strong before me!

I had asked God to make me whole again, and here she was, ready to come back to me. I looked at her and wondered if this was what I really wanted to happen. And I knew it was. I wanted to be a normal person again. With any and all parts of me working as a whole. Not broken to pieces like Humpty Dumpty. I wanted to be put back together again. I wanted to be strong and whole again.

Humpty Dumpty sat on a wall.
Humpty Dumpty had a great fall.
And all the king's horses,
And all the king's men,
Could not put Humpty together again!
—A child's nursery rhyme

The truth behind the Humpty Dumpty nursery rhyme is that Humpty did not have a choice in the matter. But I did! And I asked God to help me. And God did exactly that.

God grafted the strong branch to my side. And immediate relief flooded my soul! I had been trying to do all the things I used to do on my own, alone, cut off from my other parts. I was using up all my energy doing the things I had ordinarily done. Before. When I was all together. No wonder I was tired!

And then the Wolf, the Pretty Lady in Fancy Robes, came. And the Wolf blew my life to bits. The Spider came, and it began to spin. The Legion of Destroyers descended from the heavens and snatched up the souls of my daughter and her family. My daughter called to tell me she could no longer see me. Our daughter and her family disappeared. The lawyers we hired failed. The detectives we hired failed. Family Services failed. I failed. And I thought God had failed as well.

I had been limping along. Broken. Tired. Weak. Exhausted. Spending too much time trying to be

normal. Trying to survive. Trying to be ordinary.
When ordinary was no more.

Why is it so hard, Lord?
To be normal?
Just plain, everyday normal?
Like so many others I see?
Must I always be outside of other people's lives?
Looking in,
Wishing I could be inside as well?
Wishing I didn't have to try so hard to smile?
Wishing I could cry?

CHAPTER 7

P RESENTLY, ANOTHER BRANCH appeared before me. She had also been a part of my core self until I had pushed her aside. She too had become a piece of kindling wood after I had picked up the ax. Useless without a fire.

She had been a shy and unassuming part of me. Always young. And very close to God. It was precisely because she was close to God that I had banished her. I had been so angry at God at the time. I simply did not want her around.

This young branch had taken it upon herself to be the guardian of all my secrets. She was also the keeper of all my tears. She kept what was in the deepest parts of my heart and mind safe. Where no one could see. The Darkness. The sadness. The tangled threads. The Spider. The web. The hopelessness. The absence of Day. The absence of calling birds. The absence of God. The dreams. The tears. All of it. Everything I had tried to block out, she had kept. All of it. But I wasn't sure I liked what she was doing. So I had rid myself of her with one swing of the ax.

Did she still hold all those secrets in her heart? I didn't know. But I did know I needed her. I was so tired of trying to be ordinary when I wasn't ordinary at all. I was so tired of trying to survive. I needed to be whole again. Every part of me was important.

> *The eye cannot say to the hand, "I don't need you!" And the head cannot say to the feet, "I don't need you!" On the contrary, those parts of the body that seem to be weaker are indispensable, and the parts that we think are less honorable we treat with special honor. And the parts that are unpresentable are treated with special modesty, while our presentable parts need no special treatment. But God has combined the members of the body and has given honor to the parts that lacked it, so that there should be no division in the body, but that its parts should have equal concern for each other. If one part suffers, every part suffers with it; if one part is honored, every part rejoices with it. (1 Corinthians 12:21–26 NIV)*

And God took that young branch from the kindling pile and made it straight and tall. And covered it with fruit blossoms. And placed her before me.

> *With God, all things are possible.*
> *—Matthew 19:26 (NIV)*

Then God grafted her to my other side. And I was whole again. All the king's horses and all the king's men couldn't put me together again.

But God could.

And God did.

My life kept changing. As a whole person, I had ready access to all the little compartments I had built. And all the secrets that my secret-keeper had kept in her heart. Nothing was held back. All the memories. All the experiences. All the dreams and visions. All the nightmares. And all the tears. All of it. Everything was open. And I was no longer afraid. God was with me.

At times, after God's revelation to me, but before I knew Annie was coming home, I would let myself look into the open places I had uncovered from the hidden parts of my mind. The places that held all the memories of Annie. I would look, and I would let myself think about her.

Sometimes I even wished I could go back to the world where Annie lived. To catch a glimpse of her. Enough of a glimpse to know that she still existed. But I could not go back permanently to that world of visions and dreams. Of nightmares. Of police officers who rolled their eyes. Of lawyers who did not understand. Of private detectives who tried to understand, but could not. Of Family Services who would not help. Of judges. Of court. It was all too hurtful.

Still, sometimes I wished I could at least go back to Annie's world to sit in the sweet garden I had found there. The one place where I had felt safe. But I could not go back. The garden lay too near to the edge of Darkness. That garden was gone for me now.

Still, I longed to go at times. I had waited for God there. I had seen God there. I had been comforted by God there.

Sometimes I wish I could at least go back to the sweet garden I had found in that other world. The one place where I had felt safe.
Photo by Shannon Childress

I missed my sparrow wings from that world. They were gone too. Crushed. Ruined. My visions of flying from danger were no longer possible for me. And I wanted to weep for everything I had lost when I thought of these things.

But God was with me now. I did not need a secret garden to be with God. I did not need wings to fly to that sweet garden. I was safe with God. And I trusted that God would one day put all our lives back together. Either on earth—or in heaven.

Why had it taken me so long to understand what was for so long not understandable? It was because of the suffering! The suffering had to come first. Before all the rest. I had not understood the why of the suffering. Now I know that the suffering must come before the sun rises. Before Day comes.

I so wished I had known that Annie and her family would one day come home. But I did not know. Until I came to the end of myself. Until I asked God for forgiveness. Until I came to trust God.

And every day I had prayed:

> Now I lay *them* down to sleep,
> I pray thee Lord *their* souls to keep.
> And if *they* die before *they* wake,
> I pray thee Lord *their* souls to take.
> (adapted from Joseph Addison's "Now I Lay
> Me Down to Sleep.")

Protect them all, Lord God. The Prince of Darkness is relentless in his quest to devour souls. Relentless!

Help your people to be relentless as well, Lord God. Relentless in the war against the Prince of Darkness. Relentless in rescuing lost souls. Relentless in bringing your people the good news. The Savior is with us!

For God so loved the world that he gave his

*only Son, that whoever believes in him will not
perish, but have eternal life. (John 3:16 ESV)*

God's Son suffered and died for us. So that everlasting
life could be ours. *His* suffering had to come first.
Before all the rest.

> *He who dwells in the shelter of the Most High*
> *Will rest in the shadow of the Almighty.*
> *I will say of the Lord,*
> *"He is my refuge and my fortress,*
> *My God in whom I trust."*
> *"Surely he will save you from the fowler's snare*
> *And from the deadly pestilence.*
> *He will cover you with his feathers,*
> *And under his wings you will find refuge."*
> *Psalm 91:1–4a (NIV)*

The Son's suffering had to come first.

And as time unfolded before me, I was comforted
by God's presence, more and more.

And it was then that I saw the morning star.

It was then that I saw that all things were being
made new.

It was then that our daughter came home.

It was then that the sun rose once more,

And the fullness of Day came,

And the Darkness scattered.

And I saw the Lord coming to save us.

And in God's time, my family and I moved to
the other side
of the In-Between Time,
Straight into
the Day
and the Time After.
And what was once a nightmare,
Was no more.
The Wolf was no longer at the door.
The tangled mass of threads was gone.
The thread that I thought I needed to untangle
the mess,
I no longer needed.
It was God I needed.
God alone.
It is God we all need.
God alone.
And God is enough.
To defeat the Spider and its web,
The Owls,
The Dragon,
The Darkness,
The nightmares,
All of it.
God can and will, in his time, destroy all of it.
God is relentless!
The truth was finally revealed to me,
And Day,
Finally came.
God is relentless!

For all of us!
For all our souls!

And in God's own time, our lost daughter called:
"Mom? This is your daughter, Annie. I want to see
you. I miss you. I want to come home."

After twenty years, our daughter and her family
were finally free! Our daughter, who had been lost
to us, was finally coming home!

The Darkness is no more.
And my soul rests.
God is with us.
And that is all we need.
The thorns may remain to remind us of the
    Darkness,
But God is with us.
God's Son has come to save us!
God is all we need.

Now I lay *us* down to sleep,
I pray Thee Lord *our* souls to keep.
And if *we* die before *we* wake,
I pray Thee Lord *our* souls to take.
(adapted from Joseph Addison's
"Now I Lay Me Down to Sleep.")

But the fight for our lives is not done.
We must stay alert,
We must wear the full armor of God,

At all times.
The battle will come again.
The battle doesn't end here.
Not until the Dark Prince is fully and finally
Defeated.
Once and for all.
Other Spiders will spin.
Hundreds of other Spiders are already spinning.
They will come.
Many are already here.
And Wolves will come again,
Like the Pretty Lady in Fancy Robes.
They will all come.
Right up to our doorsteps.
The Owls will come again,
With talons sharp.
They will come for our souls.
But we need not fear the terrors of the night
Because God is with us.
God will help us!
And God is all we need!
The end is drawing near.
We must tell others.
We must tell them about everything.
Now!
Before the Prince of Darkness comes for their souls.
Before the final battle.

*Be self-controlled and alert. Your enemy the
devil prowls around like a roaring lion looking*

for someone to devour. Resist him, standing firm in the faith, because you know that your brothers [and sisters] throughout the world are undergoing the same kind of sufferings. And the God of all grace, who called you to his eternal glory in Christ, after you have suffered a little while, will himself restore you and make you strong, firm, and steadfast. To him be the power for ever and ever. Amen. (1 Peter 5:8–11 NIV)

PART II

Living in the Time After

Be gracious to me, O God,
For man tramples on me;
All day long,
An attacker oppresses me.
My enemies trample on me all day long;
For many attack me proudly.
When I am afraid,
I put my trust in you.
In God, whose Word I praise,
In God I trust; I shall not be afraid.
What can flesh do to me?
Then my enemies will turn back
In the day when I call.
This I know, that God is for me.
In God, whose Word I praise,
In the Lord, whose Word I praise,
In God I trust; I shall not be afraid.
What can man do to me?
—Psalm 56:1–4, 9–10 (ESV)

CHAPTER 8

T HEY TOOK AWAY everything from her:
Her freedom,
Her opportunity for a higher education,
Her opportunity for gainful employment,
And her opportunity to find success
in the outside world.
They took away everything from her:
Her ability to feel emotion,
Her ability to think and speak for herself,
Her extended family,
And all of her former friends.
They took away her access to the outside world:
Her mail,
Her telephone,
Permission to leave.
They took away her soul,
And all of her light,
Leaving only Darkness.
They took away her life before,
And they took away her life after.

They took away her dreams,
Leaving only nightmares.
They took away her home.
They took away her children.
They took away everyone she loved.
They took away her faith in God,
And finally,
They took away God.
They destroyed her.
They took away all that was inside,
And they took away all that was outside.
They took away her breath.
They took away her life.
They took away everything she held dear,
Leaving only nothingness.
And they got away with it!

In early spring of 2016, my daughter, Annie—who I had not heard from in nearly twenty years—called me. She called me almost exactly twenty years to the day she had told me she could no longer be a part of my life. Nearly twenty years since she had vanished. Nearly twenty years since the Owllike Creatures, with razor-sharp talons, had come for her soul.

"This is your daughter, Annie," she said. "I have been trying to reach you. I miss seeing you. I want to see you."

I was absolutely stunned! It had been two decades since the Terrible Day the Sky Turned Black. Since the skylights had fallen. Since a Legion of Owllike

Destroyers had swooped down from the heavens and snatched up the souls of my daughter, her husband, their child, and all of their children yet to come. Nearly twenty years after my daughter, her husband, their small son, and all of their children yet to come had disappeared. Nearly twenty years after the Dark Angel—the Prince of Darkness—had come to destroy our lives. First deceiving us. Then attacking our souls.

We should have known.

But we had not paid attention.

Jesus began to say to them, "See that no one leads you astray. Many will come in my name, saying, 'I am he!' and they will lead many astray. And when you hear of wars and rumors of wars, do not be alarmed. This must take place, but the end is not yet. For nation will rise against nation, and kingdom against kingdom. There will be earthquakes in various places; there will be famines. These are but the beginning of the birth pains. "But be on your guard. For they will deliver you over to councils, and you will be beaten in synagogues, and you will stand before governors and kings for my sake, to bear witness before them. And the gospel must first be proclaimed to all nations. And when they bring you to trial and deliver you over, do not be anxious beforehand what you are to say, but say whatever is given you in that hour, for it is not you who speak, but the Holy Spirit. And brother will deliver brother over to death, and the father his child, and children will rise against parents and have them put to death. And you will be hated by all for my name's sake. But the one who endures to the end will be saved. … And then if anyone says to you, 'Look, here is the Christ!' or 'Look, there he is!' do not believe it. For false Christs and false prophets will arise and perform signs and wonders, to lead astray, if possible, the elect. But be on guard; I have told you all things beforehand. "But in those days, after that tribulation, the sun will be darkened, and the moon will not give its light, and the stars will be falling from heaven, and the powers in the heavens will be shaken." (Mark 13, selected verses, ESV)

Jesus had warned us. And yet we had not seen it coming. We had not heard it coming. We had not believed Jesus's words. Until it was too late. Until the Prince of Darkness had nearly destroyed us.

Our children had fought against us: their own parents. And our children had let others scheme against us and against their children. They just let it happen. And they helped in whatever the elders told them to do to keep their extended family and their children in line.

Disciplining them with sharpness. Keeping them as prisoners. Poisoning their minds. They and their elders had schemed against their brothers and sisters, aunts and uncles, parents, and grandparents, and their own children. Offering up death prayers for each enemy—adult or child.

Their leader, a false prophet, rose up by claiming false doctrine to be real. And false miracles to be real. But only deceit had appeared. As did destruction. And death. Whole worlds had been tilted, totally upended. Skylights had crashed to the ground. Sun and moon and stars. Giant Owllike Creatures, with razor-sharp talons, had descended from the dark sky and had snatched up souls, screeching as they flapped their giant black wings over the burnt earth. And nothing remained that had been before. Nothing at all.

We had not heeded the warnings from scripture:

Be self-controlled and alert. Your enemy the devil prowls around like a roaring lion looking for someone to devour. Resist him, standing firm in your faith, because you know that your brothers and sisters throughout the world are undergoing the same kind of sufferings. (1 Peter 5:8–9 NIV)

I had not stood firm enough. I had ignored the signs. I had not wanted to see the signs. I had not wanted to hear the Owls screeching. I had not believed the words. I had not resisted because I had not believed there was anything to resist. I had not believed the warnings. And so, because I had not believed, the Pretty Lady in Fancy Robes came. And she took away everything.

Everything.
From our daughter,
And from me.
The Pretty Lady took away everything from me.
She took away my child;
She took away my grandchild.
She took away my work;
She took away my purpose for life.
She took away joy;
She took away my ability to feel anything at all.
She took away sleep at night;
And she took away peace in the morning.
She took away my family as I knew it;
And she took away my family as I had imagined it.
She took away all of my past,
And all of my present,
And all of my future as I thought it would be.
She took away color;
And left only blackness.
She took away laughter;
And left tears that refused to fall.
She took away pieces of my heart,
And slices of my soul.
She took away the world as I once knew it;
And she took away any courage I might have had
to rebuild it.
Most terrible of all,
She took away my faith.
And she nearly
Took away God.
—*Ordinarily Sarah*

Despite the warnings, despite the sufferings, despite the resistance, despite the anger I had experienced toward God, my daughter finally called me. After twenty years of Darkness, she called me.

And hearing my daughter's voice, after all those years, I asked myself, Is this really my Annie? Or is this someone pretending to be Annie, playing a game with me? A wicked trick. Is this my Annie? Or is this the Pretty Lady coming after me—again? Is this voice the beginning of a dream come true—or the beginning of another nightmare?

But my mother's heart knew her voice. I knew her breathing in and her breathing out. I knew the way she phrased her words. I knew the way her voice caught when she was nervous. I knew that pitch. I knew the distress signals in her voice. It was my Annie. She was no longer lost. She was on her way home. My Annie. She was coming home to me! After years of being gone, she was coming home! After twenty years of Darkness, she was coming home.

Our conversation was fragmented as we spoke on the phone. Choppy. Uneven. We were both anxious. Maybe even afraid. And our conversation went in a direction I had not expected. But what had I expected after all those lost years? Had I really expected that she would *ever* call me again? No. That we would ever have a somewhat normal conversation? No. Still, I wanted answers to questions I had about her disappearance. I wanted to ask her why she left. I wanted to ask her if I had been a failure as a mother.

I wanted to ask her if she had missed any of us during her absence.

But she didn't want to go there. The conversation turned out to be more what it was *not* about. It was not about where she had been all those years, why she had left us, or why she had decided to return. She simply wanted to reconnect with me.

I decided the answers to my questions could wait. I would not pressure her. I told her I loved her, I had missed her, and I was so happy that she was coming home. Then she said something strange. She said she didn't want her husband or her children to know she was contacting me. At least not yet. She wanted to keep me a secret for a while. I wanted to ask her why, but I decided not to.

After she told me she had to keep me a secret, some of the joy in the hearing of her voice left me. And for a moment, the pain and heaviness that had lodged behind my ribs and had accompanied me for the past twenty years returned. I felt something dark beginning to materialize before me. Something all too familiar. The hair on the back of my neck began to rise. I wanted to hang up. I wanted to run! But I couldn't.

All at once, the Darkness edged even closer, and it took its place directly over me, hovering, waiting to strike. Suddenly, it struck at my throat, making my words feel like rocks. I wasn't sure I could continue to speak. It squeezed at my neck. Harder. Harder still. It was pushing the sharp rocks lodged inside, outward, to the edge of my mouth. I wanted to ask her why I had to be a secret, but I could not. I wanted to ask her lots of things, but I could not. And when I finally found a narrow path for my words to escape, I simply asked her when and where she wanted to meet. She suggested a food court, inside of a mall, in a town halfway between where she lived and I lived. Then she said she wanted to see me only. No one else. I wanted to object, but she was firm.

Okay, I thought. I just want to see her. Nothing else matters. The wait will soon be over! My prayers have been answered. My Annie is coming back to me. I will do anything she wishes—as long as I can see her. The In-Between Time is over. The Time After has truly begun. And I am ready to embrace it.

CHAPTER 9

AFTER WE HUNG up, my mind began to whirl. What had I just agreed to?

I began to think about the meeting we had planned. Why were we meeting in a mall of all places? Right in the middle of a busy, noisy mall? Why weren't we meeting in her home with the rest of her family? Why couldn't she tell her children or her husband about our plans? Why had she waited for more a year to contact me? (She had just told me she had been out of her "prison" for more than a year already. Why had no one told me they had come "out"?)

Later, I found out that Annie's mother-in-law, Liz—one of my closest friends—had known for well over a year that Annie had "come out," but she had not said a word to me. Why?

I began to wonder what Annie looked like. Would I even recognize her after all these years? Would she have lines on her face? Gray in her hair? Would her brown eyes still hold the light and intensity in them that I remembered from her youth?

For sure, she would no longer be the young mother who left us. Her son, Rory, was now almost an adult. Interestingly, Annie's mother-in-law and I had seen Rory several years ago, in a fast-food restaurant where he worked part-time as a grill cook. We had decided at that time that we would pay Rory a visit together at his place of work. And so we made our plans, and within a week, we went to see him together. His two grandmas. His two grandmas who he had never met!

After arriving at the restaurant that day, we told the waitress who we were, and we asked her if she would kindly tell Rory his two grandmothers were sitting at a table and could we speak with him during his break. She went back into the kitchen and then returned with his response. He had said yes.

And so, we did meet him. A bit later. During his break. He came right over to our table at his break time, calmly shook our hands, and said, "Pleased to meet you!"

The three of us spoke for about fifteen minutes. It was terribly awkward. Still, I was grateful—and hopeful as well. Perhaps this was the beginning of the end. Perhaps they would all be released soon. And when his break time was over, we exchanged emails and telephone numbers. Liz and I each hugged him and kissed him on his cheeks. The visit was done.

Liz and I left the restaurant feeling absolutely stunned! Had what happened in that restaurant really happened? Had we really talked with our grandson? Hugged him? Kissed him? Exchanged email addresses and telephone numbers with him? Or had it all been just a dream.

And the next day, I wished it had never happened. The thorn dug deeper into my side. It hurt! And I wished our time with Rory had been a dream. I received a text from Rory the day after we had met, saying that his parents had forbidden him from seeing me again. And the words stung. I had thought that maybe seeing him could have been the beginning of the end, but Rory disappeared from our lives once more. It was not to be. The Fancy Lady had not taken her leave!

Thinking of my visit with Annie, I wondered if she would tell Rory she had called me this morning— after nearly twenty years of absence? Would she let me see him? Would I be allowed to see any of her children? And did I really want to meet Annie at the mall? She had taken so much from me. Would she take more? But then, I had nothing left. I had nothing to lose. I had already lost everything.

Everything.

And I began to wonder if she would recognize me when I got to the food court. I had grown older too. Grayer. Fuller. My mouth was surrounded with fine lines. After meeting with me, would she disappear again? Just like her son had. Was she coming merely to check me out? Would I be worthy in her eyes for more contact? Would I have to endure more brokenness? More of the Pretty Lady's wrath?

I wondered if I was truly in the Time After?

Had I been mistaken? Was I still in the In-Between Time? Is this what Day looked like? Full of fear and uncertainty? After the Darkness, was there still only Darkness? Would the Darkness stay forever?

*The Lord is close to the brokenhearted, and
saves those who are crushed in spirit.
—Psalm 34:18 (NIV)*

But I felt crushed and brokenhearted. Had I not yet completed the journey out of the In-Between Time? Had God abandoned me again? Had I mistakenly thought that God had crossed over with me into the Light that was Day? To the other side of the In-Between Time? Or not? Was it all just wishful thinking on my part?

CHAPTER 10

A FEW DAYS LATER, after speaking again with Annie, I drove to the mall where she and I had planned to meet. I arrived first, looked around, found a small white table in the food court, and sat down. But, suddenly, I wanted to run again! My entire life was about to change once more! Was I up to the task? Was I opening myself up to something wonderful—or was I opening myself up to a world of heartache? Was this indeed a part of the Time After? Or not?

Some years ago, I had put it all to rest. I had put Annie to rest. I had believed that I would never see her or any of her family again. Ever. And I had reached a place of acceptance. I would see them all someday, I had told myself, just not on *this* side of life. Never again on this side of life. It was just the way it was. Nothing could be changed. None of us could ever go back. We could only move forward. Not sideways. Not backward. Only forward. I had believed I would not see my daughter, her husband, or her children again, on this side of heaven.

Yet, now, amazingly, here I was, about to reunite with my daughter, in a new time and place. And I felt terrified! I wanted to run away! I wanted to go somewhere safe. I do not want to be in this mall! Is she really coming? Or is this a trap? Will she, just like Jesus's disciple Judas, betray me with a kiss, alerting my enemies as to who I was? Will I be taken away?

I looked furtively at my surroundings. This mall held sad memories for me. Memories of the time just *after* Annie and her family left us. For months after they left us, I had come to this mall alone to look through the windows of my favorite children's stores. For months, I had wished I could purchase sweet little outfits for Rory. Or small toys. Or little hardback books made especially for clumsy little hands. For months, I had wished that Annie and Rory and I could have been seated at a table like this in the food court—with a little meal for Rory and something tasty on a tray set out for Annie and me.

Why had I kept coming here all those months? Had I thought that perhaps one day they would just materialize before me? But today, it was only me I saw in those memories. Wandering around in the mall. Like a shadow. Annie and Rory no longer with me. No one to buy anything for. I could no longer see their faces. I could no longer hear their laughing. I could no longer reach for those fat little baby hands.

I wished we were not meeting for lunch. I wasn't hungry, and my throat was clogged with years of lumpy, unshed tears. What in the world would we talk about?

But it was too late. She was coming. I was about to see my daughter again!

And so, I waited at the little white table, keeping my eyes on the doorway by the carousel. The carousel I had wished I could have seen Rory ride on. But little Rory was gone. Little Rory would never be that toddler again. And the grown-up Rory was not coming today. "Pleased to meet you," he had said. And then he disappeared.

Only Annie was coming. My Annie, who wanted to keep me a secret from her family. But why? And I began to feel angry. Did her family still believe I was an enemy? Was that it? What was my daughter doing, coming here to see me? What was she thinking? Why was she coming?

I asked God to give me strength. I didn't know if I could pull it off. After twenty years, I didn't know if I could do it. How was I to welcome her back in my arms? She had been dead to me for many years. How could she be alive again?

Suddenly she appeared. By the door next to the carousel. She saw me, smiled, and came toward me. I, in turn, walked toward her. She looked good. Long brown hair with steaks of gray. Tall and slim. I had not remembered that she was so tall. Or so pretty.

The moment we reached each other, we hugged. She had been looking for me, and she had found me. She had come home. And I was there to welcome her.

Was this real? But how? And not knowing what to do next, we simply ordered sandwiches and coffee, sat down at our table, and began to talk as if the past twenty years had merely been a brief inconvenience. Nothing more.

At least that is what we made ourselves believe. No matter if she had been gone for twenty seasons—or twenty anything. No matter that so many members of our family had passed away during that time span—without her having said good-bye. No matter that so many new babies had been born into the family during that length of time—without her welcoming any of them.

No matter that I had not seen Rory grow up. No matter that I did not know the names of her other children. Or the color of their eyes. Or their ages. No matter that I knew nothing about them at all. We could get past this. For now, we would do something normal. Something all mothers and daughters do. We would sit at a table, in a food court, in a mall, eat sandwiches, drink coffee, and talk, as if all was well with the world. As if our lives had never been upended. As if the Pretty Lady had never come.

She had much to tell me. She told me that she and her family had been out of the "church" for more than a year, nearly two years in fact. She definitely did not want to talk about the church. She said it had not been a good experience. None of it had been good. She explained that she might talk about it when she was ready, but not on that day.

She told me that she had contact with her stepmother and her stepmother's extended family. That she and her husband and their children had actually visited all of them in Oklahoma. She told me that she and her children and husband had also been in contact with his parents and all his extended family.

And I thought, *How could this be? Why had none of these people called me? Why had none of them told me that Annie and her family had come out of that church?* (They had come out shortly after Annie's mother-in-law, Liz, and I, had visited Rory in that fast-food restaurant. Why hadn't Liz told me?)

I had thought that Annie's mother-in-law and I were friends. At the very least, we had shared the fact that our children and grandchildren had been caught up in that oppressive church. Why hadn't she called me to tell me that they had all come out?

I began to swell with anger. How could Annie not have contacted me at the same time she contacted everyone else? Was there something so terrible about me that no one could tell me what was going on?

And right then and there, a small part of me left the table, left the sandwiches and coffee, left Annie. It was as if I were suddenly someone else, standing apart, watching, listening. What was she telling me? How could she and her family have been "out" for more than a year already? Were the children in public schools then? I knew she had been homeschooling all of them. Rory had told me that. Was Annie no longer homeschooling them? Why had she and her family seen the other families but not mine? Why did she feel the need to keep me a secret from all the others?

And I wanted to flee. As far away as I could. I couldn't stay there any longer. I couldn't listen to her any longer! It was too hard. Too hurtful. It was not going to work. I should not have come!

But I could not leave. I had to make myself stay. I had to make myself listen. I had to sit with Annie. All of me! And I had to pretend that all was well. I could not leave her! She had come back to me! She needed me! I could not abandon her! She was my daughter!

But was she?

Or was she merely an apparition? Was I, perhaps, having a mental breakdown of sorts?

I decided to stay. Annie continued to speak of many things. She explained to me that everything began to "unravel" after Liz and I had gone to see Rory at the fast-food place where he worked. That same night, after Liz and I had seen him, Rory went home and told his parents about our meeting. And they promptly forbade him from seeing either Liz or me again. They hadn't left the church yet, and they were not allowed to see anyone outside their church.

Then Annie told me it was just a few months after Liz and I saw Rory that she announced to her church leader that she and her family would be leaving the group. And I did not understand the why of what she was saying. Perhaps because I had seen Rory, something rattled loose inside of her? Perhaps something inside of her broke apart? Perhaps Annie decided that she had had enough? But the reason didn't really matter. She was here now. Right in front of me!

She had left the group. She and her family had left. They all just walked out. (Apparently after much ranting and raving from their church leader, the Pretty Lady). As punishment, all of them were immediately shunned by those who remained in the church.

Annie and her family were told that they could no longer make any contact with any current members of the church. Ever. Annie's family was now dead to all members of their former church. And Annie knew that all the remaining members were also being told they could not make any contact with Annie and her family. Ever. She also knew that all the current members were being ordered to hurl curses and death prayers toward her and her family. Annie knew that all of this was taking place inside the church because she and her family had participated in shunning, curses, and death prayers toward others many times over the years.

Annie said she grieved the fact that she could no longer see the other children left inside the church. She explained that if she happened to see the older ones out and about at their places of work in the community, she had to look away. (She told me they were all allowed to work once they turned sixteen.) She was not allowed to speak to any of them if she happened to see them, and that hurt her heart.

Annie had homeschooled them all. She loved

them all. She believed the children would probably spend the rest of their lives under the control of their church leader, the Pretty Lady. But there was nothing Annie could do for them. Nothing at all. If she tried to make contact with them, she believed that she and her family would surely be harmed in some way. And the children left inside would be harmed as well. She had to walk away from those children she had loved. And so she did.

CHAPTER 11

ANNIE EXPLAINED THAT it was shortly after they had left the church that she, her husband, and their children began to reconcile with members of their extended families. The very same people Annie and her family had shunned and hurled curses and death prayers at for so many years! Annie's stepmother and family. Her husband's parents and their family! Everyone but me and my family. I did not understand. Why had she waited so long after contacting them to contact us? But I would not question her about it.

And I asked myself again, Who is this woman? Who is she? She looks like my Annie. She sounds like my Annie. But is she really Annie? And what is she saying to me? None of this makes sense to me. Nothing at all. Who did she say that she was?

Annie told me I had been enemy number one for many years—and I still was! She and her family had been taught by their church leader that I was evil. I wondered if that was the reason why Annie needed to keep me a secret. Did Annie's husband and children still believe I was a dangerous enemy? Maybe. All I knew for sure was that she could not tell anyone she was in contact with me, including any of the family members she had reconnected with. None of them knew she had made contact with me—and she wanted to keep it that way. So curious. So twisted!

How long would she keep me a secret? How long? How long, Lord? Who was this woman? What was she saying to me? Would this nightmare ever end? Where was Day? Where was the Time After I had thought we had entered?

Would the Time After turn out to be as dark as the Time In-Between? And before that, the Time Before? Was I back in Wonderland again with Alice? Had Alice and I, perhaps, gone through the looking glass together—with me being unaware of it? Would I escape the Queen of Hearts with Alice? Or would I be caught and forever have to live in Wonderland with a deck of cards, an annoying white rabbit, and a frightening looking Jabberwock?

And suddenly the story about the prodigal son from the gospel of Luke popped into my mind. Curious! Why would I think about the prodigal son after I had just been told that I had, for years, been the number one enemy of my daughter, her family, and her entire religious group? Shouldn't I be thinking about this religious group and how I would like to get my hands on them? Expose them? Destroy them?

There once was a rich farmer who had two sons. After the sons were grown, one of the sons decided to stay with his father and family and work on the family farm. The other son was rebellious and did not want to stay. He wanted to make his own way in the world. He asked his father for his inheritance, got it, and left.

Many years later, the rebellious son realized that he had not fared well in the world at all. And he missed his family. He decided to go home. He also realized that he had sinned against his father, and that he needed to ask his father for forgiveness:

> "I will set out and go back to my father and say to him: Father, I have sinned against heaven and against you. I am no longer worthy to be called your son. Make me like one of your hired men." So he got up and went to his father.

When the young man reached home, his father greeted him with joy! The rebellious son asked his father for forgiveness. And his father forgave him! No questions asked about why he had left, where he had been, or why he was coming back.

His father saw his son and was filled with compassion for him; he ran to his son, threw his arms around him, and kissed him.

Then the father had a feast in honor of his son:

> *The father said to his servants, "Quick! Bring the best robe and put it on him. Put a ring on*

his finger and sandals on his feet. Bring the fatted calf and kill it. Let's have a feast and celebrate. For this son of mine was dead and is alive again; he was lost and is found." So they began to celebrate. (Luke 15 NIV)

Why had this particular story come to my mind? Was my daughter a prodigal child? Had she returned to ask for my forgiveness? Can I forgive her? Can I love her? I am not sure if I even know her! It has been so long. A lifetime. Where has she been? How could she have been away for so long? How could she have done this to me? To all of us? And now she wants to keep me a secret? Where is her husband? Where are their children? When will this nightmare end? Who is this woman I have been speaking with? What is her name? Is not my daughter dead? How then could she be alive again? And how would it be possible to celebrate her return? All we had on our little white table in the middle of the food court were sandwiches and coffee and anxiousness and fear.

There was no celebration with Annie as she and I sat together at that table. No special gifts. Nothing at all. We just sat at that little white table at the mall and ate our sandwiches and drank our coffee. She talked. I listened. I was not so sure that I knew her.

And inside of me, I prayed.

The Lord is my rock, my fortress and my deliverer; My God is my rock, in whom I take refuge. He is my shield and the horn of my salvation, my stronghold. (Psalm 18:2 NIV)

And I asked myself, Is God truly my rock? My refuge? My shield? Where are you today, God? If you are near, tell me who this woman is.

How can I do this, God? How can I remain sitting here, across from this woman I am not sure I know? I need you here, God. You are the Light that scatters the Darkness! I need an entire nightmare scattered. I need the past twenty years scattered. Blotted out!

God is Light.
In him, there is no Darkness at all.
God is the Light of the whole world.
The true Light that illuminates all who believe
    in him.
God is the true Light that scatters the Darkness.
I believe this to be true.
But sometimes I find myself hiding.
Before the scattering has begun.
Before that which will be illuminated
Is illuminated.
What might I see after the Darkness is banished?
Something too terrible to see?
God asks too much of me.
It is too hard to move out of pain and loss.
Too difficult to move out of Darkness.
Too uncomfortable to be exposed by the Light.
Sometimes I think I will never get to the other side
Of *anything*!
But what other side?
I thought I was already there!

I thought I was already in the Time After.
Am I?
Or not?
But wherever I am, God,
I don't know how to ever get past the Darkness!
Ever!
The pain. The loss. The Darkness!
I don't know if I can ever get past it!
And sometimes I want to keep the Light covered
And hide in the Darkness.
It is easier hiding in the Darkness.
No one can find me there.
No one!
But can I hide from God?
For God is always near to me.
He has said so.
And God is Light.
He has said so.
Even in the Darkness,
God is there.
He has said so.
God is Light.
The true Light,
The Light that illuminates the entire world.
There is no Darkness where God lives.
God waits for his children to come out of the
    Darkness
And live in the Light!
Even me!
Help me get past it, God.

Past the Darkness.
Past the lie of thinking I can hide from you.
Help me get past it.
Help me be brave.
Help me go forward toward the Light.
Because
There is still a long way to go.

Help me be brave, God. When the Wolf (the Pretty Lady with Fancy Robes) appears at my door again, I need to be brave. When the Spider begins spinning again, I need to be brave. When the Owl-Looking Creatures with sharp talons come for my soul, I need to be brave. But how, Lord? I cannot go directly into your blinding Light. However, when the Prince of Darkness comes to devour me, I need to be brave. But how, Lord? I cannot go directly into your blinding Light. The Light will surely burn me.

I want to tell others of your goodness, Lord.
But still,
I am not sure what to say.
The journey into the Time After
Is not what I thought it would be.

You are the light of the world. A city on a hill cannot be hidden. Neither do people light a lamp and put it under a bowl. Instead they put it on its stand, and it gives light to everyone in the house. In the same way, let your light shine before men, that they may see your good deeds and praise your Father in heaven. (Matthew 5:14–16 NIV)

Help me be brave, Lord! Help my light shine.

When Annie and I finished eating our sandwiches, I thought she would go. I did not sense that there was more she wanted to talk about. But I was wrong. She asked if I could stay a while longer. Drink more coffee. I said yes. We bought more coffee and set two more steaming Styrofoam cups on our little white table. And I waited for her to speak.

Indeed, there was more to tell. Lots more. And as she began, I wanted to shut out the sound of her words. I wanted to cover my ears and shut out everything. What she was telling me was not good. I could not bear it. It was too much. Was the Wolf back at my doorstep? Was the Wolf about to blow my life to bits? Again?

Annie told me she and her husband were getting a divorce. There was no longer any love between them. She said they had stayed together because of the children. Annie explained that she had wanted to divorce her husband and leave the church years ago—after love left their marriage. But she believed if she left, the children would not be able to leave with her. One of the rules that the Pretty Lady had made clear from the beginning was this: "Anyone is free to leave the church, but if there are children, those children will stay."

And so Annie stayed. For years. She had not wanted to lose her children.

The Prince of Darkness had firmly planted himself inside the group. And their leader—the Pretty Lady—wore the face of a Wolf.

I was devastated by that news. All of it. Annie had wanted out of this church years ago, but she was unable to leave because she had been afraid of losing her children? The love Annie and her husband had shared in the beginning was no more. Annie and her husband were getting a divorce? How could any of this be?

It could not be! None of it! My mind could not accept any of it. Not today. Not while Annie and I were having lunch together after twenty years of separation!

What more will your Light reveal to me, God? I don't want to hear more. I don't want to see more. Your Light only brings me more pain! I cannot bear it! And the thorn digs ever deeper.

Incline your ear, O Lord, and answer me, for I am poor and needy. Preserve my life, for I am godly; save your servant who trusts in you—You are my God. Be gracious to me, O Lord, for to you do I cry all day long. Gladden the soul of your servant, for to you, O Lord, do I lift up my soul. For you, O Lord, are good and forgiving, abounding in steadfast love to all who call upon you. Give ear, O Lord, to my prayer; listen to my plea for grace. In the day of trouble I call upon you, for you will answer me. There is none like you among the gods, O Lord, nor are there any works like yours. ... Turn to me and be gracious to me; give your strength to your servant. (Psalm 86:1–8, 16a ESV)

Incline your ear, Lord God! Listen to my cry! Help me get past this, God! Help me get past this! Give me the strength I need to get past this!

And at once, it was revealed to me that this woman before me was indeed my daughter. She was real! She was my daughter! And she needed my help!

CHAPTER 12

AFTER I LEFT Annie that day at the mall, my mind whirled uncontrollably. All the way home, my mind whirled. How could I help her? How could I help my daughter? She had just told me she would be going to court in a few short months. A judge would decide who would have custody of the children. She was worried. *Why is she worried? Why does a judge need to make that decision? Couldn't Annie and her husband make that decision for themselves?*

Annie had also told me that her husband had an array of witnesses ready to testify on his behalf. Annie had no witnesses. I told her I would be happy to speak for her. She told me it was too late for her lawyer to schedule any witnesses. How could that be? I did not understand. She had raised the children. She had homeschooled the children. She had protected the children. Why was there any question as to who should have custody of the children? But she was worried. And suddenly, so was I.

What if she lost the children?

Her lawyer had told her not to worry. That it would all turn out okay. The judge would make a decision in her favor. But Annie was not so sure. And neither was I. Something dark began niggling at me. Something in the shadows. I couldn't define "it," but "it" was there all the same. Something was going on. Something named "it." And I couldn't fight "it" because I did not know what "it" was.

This something began swirling above me, cold, damp. It began swishing over my feet, like water. It began circling about my body, like a wrench, closing in on me tighter and tighter. Then this something began to push me forward, further, and further still. Why was it pushing me further and further into the Darkness? Where did it come from? Why was it here? What did it want from me?

I didn't know. But I was afraid. For my daughter. For the children. For me. And I did not know what to do.

I encouraged Annie to ask her lawyer if I could go with her to their next meeting. I wanted to talk to him. Maybe I could be helpful to her in that way. Anyway, I wanted to hear him say to her—and to me—why she should not worry. I wanted to hear him say to her—and to me—that he was sure she would get custody of her children. She had protected them while they had experienced abuse from church leadership. Annie told me there had been abuse toward both the adults and the children. For years, she had taken the brunt of the abuse for her children. The brunt of the punishments. There should be no question. She should have custody of them.

I did go with her when she next met her lawyer. About a month before the actual trial date.

Her lawyer was late for our appointment. And he was in a hurry. It seemed as if he did not really want to spend any more time with us than he absolutely had to. I noticed right away that he was very unorganized. His papers spilled out of his briefcase in a haphazard way as he tried to retrieve them. And he looked like he had just rolled out of bed: unshaven, unruly hair, wrinkled shirt. He was also overweight, sweaty, and out of breath. As if he had just run up four flights of stairs.

He was also rude. He barely acknowledged my existence in the room.

Hoping to save time during our meeting with Annie's lawyer, I had written to him ahead of our meeting regarding many of the abuses that Annie and the children had endured over the years from the leadership of their former church. (One would think, since I had communicated with him, that Annie's lawyer would have acknowledged me, but he barely glanced my way!) I had also written to him that I was especially concerned for the children because at one time, Annie's husband, Bret, had been in a position of leadership in the church (although I had no idea if Bret had ever physically hurt Annie or the children). I thought it would be helpful for Annie's lawyer to know that Annie had tried to shield her children from the church leadership as best as she could over the years—however many people that included.

I had also written that I was concerned that Bret's brother was still a leader in the church and that the church continued to meet for worship across the street from the home where Bret and Annie and all of their children had lived for years. If Bret was awarded custody of the children, they would continue to live in that house. So, wouldn't it be better for the children to live with their mother some distance away—where they would not be in such close proximity to the church, its leaders, their uncle, their aunt, all their cousins, and all the painful memories associated with life in that church?

But again, her lawyer barely glanced my way.

Bottom line, even though I had sent him several pages of valuable information, he barely glanced at me. He was rude to me. Maybe he had not yet read the material I had sent him? Or maybe he had read it but didn't know what to do with the information? What had he been doing? Was he lazy? Or terribly unorganized? Or totally incompetent?

I had also sent Annie's lawyer a list of about a dozen people who could be witnesses on behalf of Annie and her struggle to protect her children while inside the church. This list included two child welfare workers who had investigated allegations of abuse and neglect within the church, a retired cop who had spent some time investigating the church and allegations of abuse inside of it, a private detective, whom I had hired to investigate allegations of abuse inside the church, a lawyer, whom I had hired to bring allegations of abuse inside the church to court, and several former members of the church (who had left the church and had told me and my private detective that there had been abuse inside the church waged against adults and children alike.)

I also wrote to Annie's lawyer explaining to him that although these potential witnesses had told me they had all done investigative work on my behalf, I was not sure what they actually had accomplished. They all seemed to keep any findings they had accumulated close to their vests. And although all of these people had tried to help me get the children out of that church, they had all failed. Eventually, Annie and her family escaped—of their own accord.

Annie's lawyer never responded to me about the witness list I sent him. Perhaps, if I had been in his place, I would be sweating too! How embarrassing! And when I asked him if it was really too late for me to be a witness on Annie's behalf—Bret had at least half a dozen witnesses on his behalf, and Annie had none—he told me it was too late. No one could be a witness for Annie. It was too late. End of story. Not up for discussion.

At that point, I really began to worry. What was he doing? I knew he had taken Annie's case pro bono—at least sort of—but I also knew he was getting paid something by someone. (I don't believe he was aware that Annie and I knew he was getting paid.) Regardless, weren't lawyers supposed to do their job?

And I couldn't help but ask myself if someone from the "other side" was paying him *not* to do his job? Why else would he *not* want information that could help Annie? Since there was no way I would be able to find that out, Annie and I had to keep listening to him saying, over and over again, "Don't worry. You will get the children."

Was he really so sure about the outcome? Or did he know there was, indeed, another outcome rising up, and he didn't want to tell us what it was? Had the Pretty Lady in Fancy Robes gotten to him?

By the time we left the office, I was disgusted. How could there be any justice without all the facts?

I suddenly felt like I was inside the children's tale of the Three Little Pigs. The first little pig had shaken with fear inside his house of straw while the Big Bad Wolf was crouching outside and screaming, "Little pig! Little pig! Let me in! Or I'll huff. And I'll puff. And I'll blow your house in!"

The little pig became frightened for his life! He knew his house of straw was no match for the Wolf at the door! What to do? What to do? And the little pig ran away to his brother's house.

I wondered if Annie's lawyer sensed the Wolf at his own door. Was her lawyer going to run away too? Was he already running away?

I was becoming more and more concerned for my daughter—and for myself. I didn't know if I could go through more of this never-ending nightmare! It was too much! The Wolf was at our door, and in short order, our lives could be blown to bits! But what could I do? Annie's lawyer did not seem to be interested in helping her. He would not even consider the information I had given him concerning Annie's plight. And I would not be allowed to be a witness! Was this lawyer in league with the Wolf? Was he being paid "thirty pieces of silver" by the Wolf? Was our defense then going to be nothing more than straw?

Help us, God! Give us strength. Give us courage. Give us calm. The Wolf is at the door.

"Holy Mary, Mother of God, show me what to do!" I muttered. "You are a mother, and you suffered when your Son was dragged away and offered up to the religious leaders, the soldiers, and the teachers of the law. How did you survive? How did you get through your Son's beatings? The mocking? The blood! The slow walk to the cross! The hammering! The hanging! The death! How did you get through all of that? Tell me how you did it, Mary! You knew he was innocent. And you couldn't help him.

Did you see the Wolf sneering at you, Mary? Did you see him sneering at your Son?

But you held your ground. You did not leave your Son's side. You did not run away.

Mary's Son, Jesus, had also faced the Wolf. A few days before his death, as he led his disciples into Jerusalem for the last time, he knew his time had come. He saw the Wolf. He knew no one would be able to help him. He knew his life would soon be blown to bits! How had he remained calm when he knew what was before him? How had he retrieved enough strength get past his last days, knowing that he was about to lose his life?

> *"We are going up to Jerusalem," he [Jesus] said (to his disciples); "and the Son of Man will be betrayed to the chief priests and teachers the law. They will condemn him to death and will hand him over to the Gentiles, who will mock him and spit on him, flog him and kill him." (Mark 10:33–34a NIV)*

As Jesus was speaking to his disciples during those last days, he knew that his words were confusing and frightening. Would they remember all he had taught them? Would they remember the prayers he had prayed for them? Would they remember anything at all? In time, would they build flimsy lives for themselves? Would they run when the Wolf came—or would they build strong lives and stand their ground when the Wolf appeared?

Was Jesus frightened as he journeyed to Jerusalem? Was he wondering if he would be able to endure the coming days?

Jesus was living a nightmare, but he kept it to himself. No one knew except for the Wolf. And his Father, who was God. Was there any way Jesus could get past the Darkness? He set his face like stone and pushed forward. He did not ask his disciples for help. He did not ask his mother for help. He asked no one, save his Father, for help. He just kept going.

He [Jesus] set his face to go to Jerusalem.
—Luke 9:51 (ESV)

He simply put one foot in front of the other. Over and over again. All the way to Jerusalem. Jesus was relentless in doing what he had to do!

A few days later, in Jerusalem, on the night just after Jesus and his disciples had their last meal together, they went to the garden. Jesus knew he had only a short time before his arrest. He knew one of his disciples would betray him. He knew his death was imminent. And he knew the Wolf was standing near to him. The Wolf was relentless in his quest to destroy Jesus. The Wolf stood so close that Jesus could smell his foul breath, but Jesus did not run. He did not hide. Jesus stood his ground. He simply knelt down—while his disciples were sleeping—and prayed.

The Wolf was relentless in his quest to destroy
Jesus. And now
the Wolf stood so close that Jesus
could smell his foul breath.
Kris Stoyer, graphic artist

Jesus knew that his Father was all he had. But his
Father was all he needed.

*Jesus went out as usual to the Mount of Olives,
and his disciples followed him. On reaching the
place, he said to them, "Pray that you will not fall
into temptation." He withdrew about a stone's
throw beyond them, knelt down, and prayed,
"Father, if you are willing, take this cup from
me; yet not my will, but yours be done." An angel
from heaven appeared to him and strengthened*

him. And being in anguish, he prayed more earnestly, and his sweat was like drops of blood falling to the ground. When he rose from prayer and went back to the disciples, he found them asleep, exhausted from sorrow. "Why are you sleeping?" he asked them. "Get up and pray so that you will not fall into temptation." (Luke 22:39, 41–46 NIV)

Jesus was willing to follow his Father's plan instead of his own. Would any of us be so obedient to God if he asked us to go into dark places? Would any of us be able to pray, as Jesus did, "Not my will but yours?" Would we be able to pray so hard that our sweat would flow like drops of blood? Would we be willing to pray for others during our time of distress? Would we be willing to do God's will with the Wolf breathing into our faces?

Sometimes I wonder how any of us get through dark places. I wonder how any of us get to the other side of the Darkness. And the answer? We get to the other side only through Jesus! Jesus is the Day!

Jesus got to the other side. But first, he suffered and died. Then he became Day—for the rest of us.

Must we also suffer and die?
Must suffering and dying come first,
Before we find Day?
And the answer,
Sometimes,

Is Yes.
And Yes.
Some are called to suffer.
All are called to die to themselves.
Some are called to understand the "why" of it
In order to bring the good news
To those who are suffering.
To tell others who suffer
That God is near to them,
And God is all
Any of us
Need.
For God
Is Day.

The Lord is my rock, my fortress, and my deliverer; my God is my rock in whom I take refuge. He is my shield and the horn of my salvation, my stronghold. I call to the Lord, who is worthy of praise, and I am saved from my enemies. The cords of death entangled me; the torrents of destruction overwhelmed me. The cords of the grave coiled around me; the snares of death confronted me. In my distress I cried to my God for help. From his temple he heard my voice; my cry came before him, into his ears. (Psalm 18:2–6 NIV)

He reached down from on high and took hold of me; he drew me out of deep waters; He rescued me from my powerful enemy. From my foes, who were too strong for me. They confronted me in the day of my disaster, but the Lord was my support. He brought me out into a spacious place; he rescued me because he delighted in me. (Psalm 18:16–19 NIV)

I can get to the other side of Darkness as long as God stays near. As long as I ask God to stay near, I can get through my daughter's divorce. I can get through my daughter losing her children. I can get through the nightmares and the tears. I can get through whatever Darkness the Wolf sends me. I can get through it. Until God scatters the Darkness. And Day comes.

One of the Wolves who was subjecting me to the Darkness was Annie's lawyer. I decided I would stand my ground and fight that Darkness. I shared with Annie's lawyer more background information about "the church" that I thought he could use during Annie's trial. I told him that, years ago, she had been ordered by church leadership to cut off all ties with her past. Including her family. Her friends. Her possessions. Anything at all that connected her to her past life. It all had to be destroyed. Anything. Everything. Her entire life from before had to be wiped away. She had to become a new person. Receive a new identity. Her life before would no longer exist.

They killed her identity.

They killed her soul.

And they got away with it.

I had also explained to Annie's lawyer how—as a result of that order to cut off all ties with her past—Annie and Bret and their children were, from that day forward, forever denied access to anyone they had previously known. That caused much suffering and pain for Annie and Bret, for their children, and for their children to come—as well as for all of their extended family members and all of their former friends who still lived in the outside world.

It all had begun on the Day the Sky Turned Black, the skylights fell down, and the Owls came for their souls. That was the day Annie was forced to obey her leader's order. Her leader sometimes wore a pretty face and dressed up in fancy robes, but at other times, she wore the face of a Wolf.

I told Annie's lawyer the repercussions of that order—and the nightmare that followed—would continue for a lifetime. For all of us.

Her lawyer simply responded by telling Annie not to worry. And as he tried to smile at her with assurance, I thought I saw his lips curl. I thought, for a moment, he was wearing the face of a Wolf. I thought I could see the Spiders spinning their webs inside of him. And I thought I saw Owls, with sharp talons, flying away with his soul.

He did not do anything for Annie.

And he got away with it.

CHAPTER 13

I ALSO TOLD ANNIE'S lawyer that, for many years, I had been relentless in trying to rescue her and her family from the cultlike church. I had contacted the police in two different police departments. I had contacted various agencies that helped at-risk children. I had contacted other parents and grandparents who had children and grandchildren involved with this oppressive church. I had contacted several lawyers. I had contacted individuals who had been members of the church at one time. I had contacted a private investigator. I had even contacted the FBI. Unfortunately, no one was able to help very much.

It seemed as if the pain and suffering my daughter and her children had experienced were beyond the reach of the law. In most states, including the one we lived in, grandparents had no right to see their grandchildren. We were unable to help our daughter and her family in any way. Also, because all the adults involved with the church had, allegedly, joined the church of their own volition, there was nothing we could do to get the adults out either. There were crimes that had been committed—but nothing we could prove. Allegations of child abuse were investigated, but since no bruises were found on the children, the investigations were halted. Lastly, the church was not investigated rigorously because the rule of law in our country makes a clear separation between church and state.

Annie's lawyer did not seem to be interested in what I had to say.

I told Annie's lawyer that she and her family had suffered in various ways. Phone calls were prohibited (both incoming and outgoing). Gifts of any kind from parents or grandparents to church members were prohibited. Letters were prohibited (both incoming and outgoing). Any mail that did get through was intercepted and destroyed by church leadership. Also, warnings were made by church leadership to those in the outside world who would dare take it upon themselves to "trespass" on church members' property. Further, those from the outside world were not welcome in the Fancy Lady's church or in church members' homes. It was the church's standing policy that any insiders or outsiders who disobeyed these "rules" would be punished—or even prosecuted.

Annie's lawyer did not seem to be interested in anything I had to say.

Were there no laws that could help these church members escape their nightmares? Apparently not. Were there no laws that would allow parents and grandparents to see their estranged children and grandchildren? Apparently not. Were there no laws that could protect these children? Apparently not.

The church leadership took away everything.

Everything.

And they got away with it.

Did Annie's lawyer show no interest in what I had to tell him because he knew that what I had to say would not make any difference in the case? Annie had chosen of her own volition to join and stay in the church. And as her children were born, she had even more reason to stay. She stayed to protect her children.

Annie had protected her children. But did her lawyer care? Would a judge care? She had taken care of them. Homeschooled them. Protected them. Under the most horrendous of circumstances. But would any of those facts make a difference in the judge's final decision as to who would receive custody of the children?

Later, I would find out the answer: "No!"

Would the judge take away Annie's children?

"Yes."

Would the judge take away Annie's life as she knew it?

"Yes."

Could the Wolf enter the courtroom?

"Yes."

Could the Wolf participate in the proceedings?

"Yes."

Had the face of the judge became like that of a

Wolf as she made her pronouncement? "The children will go to their father."

"Yes."

And the judge got away with it.

They all got away with it!

Later, I found out that a Wolf had absolutely entered the courtroom. And I would not able to do a thing about it. I would not even be allowed to be a witness for my daughter.

There was more I shared with Annie's lawyer. I told him that Annie and her children had been held as virtual prisoners for twenty years. That very seldom had they been allowed out of their house (with the exception of their backyard, around which a huge privacy fence had been built). Annie did tell me that she and her children had been allowed to go to the local park on occasion, with a group from her church, and that they had been allowed to go to a restaurant, on occasion, as a church group. Also, Annie had been allowed to go to the grocery store to get food and other supplies. But that was it. Except for going to worship services. (They were all required to go to worship services.)

However, for all practical purposes, the children, and Annie, were isolated from the rest of the world until the day they walked out.

None of this seemed to interest Annie's lawyer. At all. None of it seemed to matter. Apparently, none of it was illegal. I wondered how being held as virtual prisoners for years and years could be legal.

The church and its leaders stole the lives of my daughter and her family.

The church and its leaders stole my life as well. And my husband's life. And the lives of everyone else in our family.

And they got away with it!

All of them got away with it!

The Wolf had come right through their church doors many years before and had waited patiently for moments of disobedience, rebelliousness, or betrayal to occur. The Wolf had waited for each misstep. It had waited for any sign of weakness. It had waited for church members to fall. The Wolf had waited for these opportunities to pounce. To destroy. To kill.

And shiny black Spiders—unseen and in league with the Wolf—had woven their Spider traps to lure their victims into their webs, one by one. For the soulless bodies that were left. For final consumption.

Why, O Lord, do you stand far off? Why do you hide yourself in times of trouble? In his arrogance the wicked man hunts down the weak, who are caught in the schemes he devises. (Psalm 10:1–2 NIV)

He [the wicked one] lies in wait like a lion in cover; he lies in wait to catch the helpless; he catches the helpless and drags them off in his net. His victims are crushed, they collapse; they fall under his strength. (Psalm 10:9–10 NIV)

The Wolf enters and waits. He waits for the right moment. And then he strikes. Without mercy. And devours heart, minds, and souls. The Spiders spin their webs. And catch and eat their soulless victims. Without mercy.

And the worst of it? Annie and her family had no idea that the god they worshipped was a counterfeit god. They were worshipping a false idol, a Pretty Lady in Fancy Robes, who claimed to be god. If only they had known that the real God was near. That after the suffering, and the dying, life and hope would return.

Now I lay *them* down to sleep,
I pray Thee Lord *their* souls to keep.
And if *they* die before *they* wake,
I pray Thee Lord *their* souls to take.
(adapted from Joseph Addison's "Now I lay me down to sleep.")
I want to see them on the other side, God.
All of them.
I want to see them
on the other side.
Hold them.
Kiss them.
Tell them I love them.
Tell them they are loved by me,
And everyone else in the family.
Tell them God is near.
The real God.
The God who loves them

And will make a home for them
And will take care of them,
Forever!

I also gave Annie's lawyer a list of all the other things that she had been denied over the years. She was denied educational opportunities post high school. Annie had started at the university in the fall following her high school graduation, but she did not do well. She managed to finish her first year (barely), but she dropped out after the first semester of her second year. She was miserable. Her grades were poor. She had no friends. She acted distant toward her friends and family. The only person she seemed to care about was her then-to-be husband, Bret, and the people in the small congregation she and Bret were attending.

I had been happy that she was attending a church regularly—and that she had a boyfriend—but something was off. Something was very off. And when she dropped out of school, I was not terribly surprised. Disappointed. But not surprised. She did not want to be in school.

And it was after my daughter came home, after twenty years of being imprisoned by her church, that Annie told me it was the leader of her church, the Pretty Lady in Fancy Robes, who had told her to drop out of school. Annie was told that she did not need to remain in school. That the church would teach her all she needed to know.

Annie also told me that she was also denied any

independent thinking. (No wonder their leader did not want their members to attend schools of higher education!) Annie told me that she and any others who tried to think independent thoughts of any kind were punished! The members were told that their leader, the Pretty Lady, could read their minds and knew exactly what they were thinking. Therefore, if anyone was caught thinking anything other than what was taught to them by church leadership, they would be punished. She also told me she was excoriated many times by church leadership for allegedly thinking independent thoughts.

The Wolf was eating the hearts and minds and souls of all the people—and the Spiders kept spinning. And trapping.

Annie said she was never allowed to have any emotions. She could not show sadness. She could not show joy. Emotions were simply not allowed. And if she was caught showing feelings of any kind, she would most likely be accused of having an evil spirit inside of her and would have to undergo an exorcism. She told me she endured many exorcisms during the early years. But she told me she learned to control her feelings in later years in order to avoid punishments. She told me she became masterful at controlling her emotions. Annie said that because of this rule, she was never allowed to enjoy her pregnancies and was never allowed to fully enjoy raising her children. When she lost one of her children during the birthing of him, she was not allowed to show any emotion of sadness or grief at all. Not a shred. She was told she must have done something terrible, and her punishment was the death of her child. And when she could not contain her grief, she was punished.

The Wolf was running rampant inside the church. And the Wolf was eating the hearts and minds of all the people in the church.

Annie told me she was never allowed any opportunities for gainful employment. All those years she was expected to take care of her family, have babies, homeschool her children, keep the house clean, tend the garden, cook, attend worship, and obey all of the church's rules. No work outside of the house was allowed. She was a prisoner for all those years. Locked away in that house.

> They took away everything from her.
> Her feelings.
> Her basic human rights.
> Her children.
> Her life.
> And they got away with it.
> And she had no one to help her.
> No parents,
> No siblings,
> No grandparents,
> No friends.
> And in her mind,
> No God.

Annie also explained to me how she would have to find gainful employment somewhere after the divorce was final. She would have to find a way to support herself and her children. But what could she do? She had no education, no work experience, and little to no knowledge about how to function in the outside world. If Bret got custody of the children, he and the children would live in the house they had all shared for more than twenty years. She would have to leave! And she would have nowhere to go! Nowhere at all! There would be no home for her.

> Would the law,
> as well as the church,
> take everything from her?
>
> How was she to live?
> She had nothing,
> save the children.
>
> If the courts took away the children,
> she would have nothing,
> Nothing at all.

The Wolf had stolen most everything she had. Would the court steal the rest of it—and get away with it?

At some point during her imprisonment, Annie began to realize that she was being deceived. She was imprisoned, stolen from, dragged down, and lied to. She had no control of any part of her life. The Wolf, the Spiders, and the Dark Angel (the Pretty Lady) were in control.

The Dark Angel had disguised herself—for all those years—as a Pretty Lady in Fancy Robes. She had proclaimed to her followers that she was God's mouthpiece. She claimed she was the chief messenger for God. She had proclaimed to her followers that they needed to obey her or be punished. She had proclaimed to her followers that they must bow down to her and worship her. This Dark Angel was in league with the Prince of Darkness.

This Dark Angel destroyed my daughter—and got away with it. She got away with murder.

> *Come to me, all you who are weary and burdened, and I will give you rest. Take my yoke upon you and learn from me, for I am gentle and humble in heart, and you will find rest for your souls. For my yoke is easy, and my burden is light. (Matthew 11:28–30 NIV)*

Help Annie, Lord God.
She needs you.
She doesn't know it yet.
But she needs you.
Open her eyes, Lord,
So she can
See
You.

I also explained to Annie's lawyer how, over the years, Annie had been forced to hurl curses at my husband and me. She was also forced to pray death prayers toward us. Their leader showed her how. Showed them all how. All of them. Both children and adults. The church leader showed them all how to call on the winds of the north, south, east, and west to bring curses and death to whomever they wished.

I still sometimes wonder whether any of the curses and death prayers had any real power. All I can say is that during a very short period of time, I lost my father, my mother, my sister, my brother-in-law, my sister-in-law, two beloved pets, and five grandchildren (due to four miscarriages and a stillbirth). Was this normal? Did other families go through so many deaths in such a short period of time? I did not know.

I told Annie's lawyer that, perhaps worst of all, she had told me that her children witnessed and took part in all of the cursing and death-praying, Annie had been forced into uttering curses and praying death prayers over her own children's heads when they disobeyed church rules! The children had endured years of these curses and death prayers. And they had endured being told that they were wicked. They were whores. They were bitches. They were witches. They were full of demons. How would the children ever get past all the verbal abuse—let alone all the physical abuse?

Annie's lawyer did not seem to believe me. Either

that or he did not want to believe me. Was the fix in? Was someone paying him to lose the case? I began to wonder. And whenever I looked at his face, I saw the outline of the face of a Wolf.

CHAPTER 14

ONE DAY IN late 2014, they all walked out—but I did not know it until more than a year later. They were out, but they made no contact with me at all. During that year, they made contact with Annie's stepmother and her large extended family and with Bret's mother and father and their large extended family. I had no idea at all that any of this was happening until early 2016, a little more than a year after they had walked out.

Today, nearly three years after my daughter contacted me, I wonder if Annie and her children will ever be able to get past the Darkness they endured. Are their wounds still tucked deep inside of them? Will the children ever be able to transition from cursing and praying for the deaths of others to a brand-new world where doing and saying those things is unacceptable? Will they ever be able to get past their own parents praying death prayers over their own heads? Will they forever think that was a perfectly normal thing to do? Will they do the same thing over their children's heads one day? Will they be able to escape the Wolves that will come to the doors of their homes someday? Will the Wolves come for their children?

> For now,
> There are no answers.
> There are only questions
> And prayers
> And hope.
> Hope
> That one day, things will get better.
> Hope
> That one day
> They will find
> Day!

Annie and her children endured unspeakable things over the years, including especially brutal punishments that I also shared with her lawyer.

An adult, or a child, about to be punished, would often be placed inside a circle of church members in the front part of their worship space. The blinds would be shut tight, and the curtains drawn, so that very little light could enter the space. The subject in the middle of the circle would often have to wear a mask or a bag over their head. The church members, hand in hand, would begin to circle the subject. Around and around they would go, chanting as they circled, mocking, shaming, and cursing them—over and over and over again.

Ring-a-round the rosies,
A pocket full of posies,
Ashes! Ashes!
We all fall down!
—A children's nursery rhyme

The Dark Angel's (the Pretty Lady's) appointed preacher at a worship service would scream, shout, point, condemn, growl, and even hit or kick members, including children if he felt that certain ones needed to be punished. Most of the worship would take place in semidarkness—and it could go on for hours.

If children misbehaved, they would be made to stand in corners, against walls, or in front of the church facing the rest of the members for very long periods of time. The children were often frightened, and they cried and screamed in fear. Sometimes they were forced to strip down to their underwear. Sometimes they were stripped down to nothing at all and spanked on their bare bottoms.

Both children and adults were threatened with curses or death—and even death by fire—if they refused to obey church rules.

Both children and adults were forced to chant death prayers and curses at extended family members. All extended family members outside their church were classified as evil persons. They were all listed on the Pretty Lady's enemy list. I was listed as enemy number one.

Children and adults both were forced to cut

up pictures of extended family members. I don't understand when this happened since Annie had told me that she had to get rid of all her possessions that connected her to her past, including all of her childhood picture albums. I don't know—and I don't want to ask her at this point. However, I have seen these albums, and sure enough, scores of pictures are either missing or cut up. Sometimes entire bodies of people, including family and former friends, are cut out of the photographs. The most eerie thing, however, is that many of the remaining photographs had heads missing. Annie told me that she and her children were ordered to cut off the heads of their grandparents: Al and me. Chilling! Absolutely chilling! And what did she tell her children as they cut off our heads? I am not sure if I ever want to know.

At times, parents were ordered to shave off all the hair from their children's heads as punishment for whatever rule the child might have broken. I asked Annie if she had ever done it, and she said yes because she had been ordered to do so. She had to obey all the Dark Angel's orders. I can't even begin to think of that terrible image of Annie and her children.

Annie told me that most of the children who belonged to that church were eventually "disowned" by their parents as they grew up and began to question the practices of the church.

She also told me that, on occasion, grown children were asked to disown their parents. And they often did.

Young children were taught to sit motionless throughout long worship services. If they moved even a little bit, they were immediately punished for their horrible sin.

Parents were forced to watch their children being punished by church leaders. Annie told me that the leaders were very careful to place bruises in places where others would not see them: under their shirts, high up on their legs, or under their pants.

Sometimes, as described earlier, the children were made to strip down to their underwear or even stand naked, and they were slapped and/or beaten on their buttocks—usually in the front part of the church and the other members.

At least one of the children was locked up in a dog cage when she disobeyed the rules. Another child was thrown across the room and stomped on by the preacher.

How did these children survive? And how will they ever erase these cruel memories from their minds? How will they ever get past the horrors of their punishments?

The Dark Angel (the Pretty Lady) wrote a manifesto for all her church members to follow. This manifesto had to be followed to the letter, by all. If any member broke even one of the rules, they were told they would be consumed by fire.

The Dark Angel religiously read the obituary page in the local newspaper. If she discovered that someone she had prayed a death prayer for had died, she would brag about how she had brought death to one of her enemies. Then she would want to celebrate—and all of her followers were forced to celebrate with her. There were many such celebrations.

Any members who left the church were threatened and intimidated by the Dark Angel and others in church leadership by mail or phone. These defectors were ordered to keep their mouths shut about their experiences in the church or risk being consumed by fire.

Perhaps the worst thing that happened to Annie surrounds the birth of her fifth child. When Annie went into labor, she was told that she could not go to the hospital until she had been exorcised from a particularly fearsome spirit. As Annie's labor progressed and she experienced more and more pain, the Dark Angel doubled down and told her she absolutely could not go to the hospital until the troublesome spirit was gone. Annie told me she became increasingly fearful as the minutes became hours. She told me she could feel that her baby was in distress, and she became more and more sure, as the hours went by, that her baby was moving less and less.

Finally, the baby stopped moving altogether. And Annie believed that her baby had died. By the time the Dark Angel allowed Annie to go to the hospital, the baby was indeed lifeless. And she had to deliver her dead baby. The doctor told her if she had gotten to the hospital sooner, he would have been able to save the little boy. Annie did not tell the doctor why she had not come sooner. No one did. The Dark Angel (the Pretty Lady) had gotten away with murder. Again! This time, she had gotten away with a physical murder!

After Annie lost her baby, she was sick with grief. She was sick that she had not been allowed to go to the hospital when she needed to. She was sick that she would be unable to bring any charges against the Dark Angel. It would be a case of "she said, she said," and Annie felt it would be impossible to win. There it was. Her baby was dead. The Dark Angel had killed her baby, but Annie had no way to prove it. The Dark Angel had prevailed. The Dark Angel always prevailed.

The Dark Angel was very clear about how Annie was to behave after the baby was lost. The Pretty Lady told Annie that the baby's death was God's judgment upon her because of Annie's wickedness. And under no circumstances was Annie to grieve for the child. Not one tear. For if she showed any emotion at all about the child, it meant that the loathsome spirit was still inside of her.

And that is where it all ended for that child. His mother could not mourn for him. His brothers and sisters could not mourn for him. His father could not mourn for him. There would be a brief graveside service at the cemetery, and the baby would be buried in a borrowed grave that belonged to the family of the Dark Angel. The Dark Angel would preside over the short service. After it was completed, no one would be allowed to speak of the baby ever again. His short life ended before it could begin. The Pretty Lady took it from him.

The Dark Angel (the Pretty Lady in Fancy Robes) got away with it! She got away with murder!

Astonishingly, when Annie went into labor with her sixth child, she bravely made her way to the hospital alone—without telling anyone. She knew her baby would be safe in the hands of the hospital staff, and she gave birth to a healthy little girl.

The very last thing I told Annie's lawyer was that I had nearly seventeen years' worth of journals covering my experiences in trying to get Annie and her family out of the church. I also had numerous legal documents, letters, and copies of hundreds of emails between myself and my private investigator. Still, the lawyer never said a word to me about anything I had given him. He seemed not to care. None of it seemed to matter to him. None of it at all.

Lord God, help my daughter. It is all too wretched. Too sad. Too horrible. Too evil. It is just too much, Lord. How will she ever get past it? How will her children ever get past it? How will my extended family ever get past it? How will my other children—now adults with children of their own—get past it? My husband? Aunts, uncles, grandparents, others? Me? Where is justice, Lord God? Where is justice for your children?

Why does the Almighty not set times for judgment? Why must those who know him look in vain for such days? Men move boundary stones; they pasture flocks they have stolen. They drive away the orphan's donkey and take the widow's ox in pledge. They thrust the needy from the path and force all the poor of the land into hiding. Like wild donkeys in the desert, the poor go about their labor of foraging food; the wasteland provides food for their children. They gather fodder in the fields and glean in the vineyards of the wicked.

The groans of the dying rise from the city, and the souls of the wounded cry out for help. But God charges no one with wrongdoing. There are those who rebel against the light, who do not know its ways or stay in its paths. When daylight is gone the murderer rises up and kills the poor and needy; in the night he steals forth like a thief.

In the dark, men break into houses, but by day they shut themselves in; they want nothing to do with the light. For all of them, deep Darkness is their morning; they make friends with the terrors of the Darkness.

But God drags away the mighty by his power; though they become established, they have no assurance of life. He may let them rest in a feeling of security, but his eyes are on their ways. For a little while they are exalted, and

*then they are gone; they are brought low and
gathered up like all others; they are cut off like
heads of grain. (Job 24:1–6, 12–14, 16–17,
22–24 NIV)*

Where is justice when the powerful have their way,
God? When the powerful are infested with Spiders
and their faces look like the faces of Wolves? When
the powerful encourage Owllike Creatures to fly
down from the night sky to capture the souls of their
victims? Where is justice?

Many do not know
Where justice can be found.
They think it only comes
From other people,
Powerful people.
But they are wrong!

Real justice comes only at the hands of God.
God can defeat evil,
With merely a word,
Or by sending his angels to fight,
Clothed with armor, helmets, and swords.
God can send plagues,
Or drought.
Famine,
Or fire,
Or floods,
Or whatever God chooses to fight with.

Only God can defeat Satan.
And God will,
In the end,
Defeat Satan,
By bringing Satan's power totally to an end.
When God's Son returns.
When will that be?
No one knows but God.
Not even God's own Son.
Should we feel hopeless then?
As we wait?
No!
Never!
God wants us all to help in the fight,
To recognize and wipe out evil wherever we can.
We are not helpless,
And we are not without hope.
If only more knew,
About God's justice,
About God's power.
About our role in defeating the enemy.
Does the Evil One know he is doomed—
And that his time is growing short?
Yes!
That is why he is working so hard,
Here and now,
To destroy us!

I wonder if all the Wolves at people's doors know
they can never be strong enough to defeat God and

God's army of angels. A single breath from God can blow away all the Dark Angels, all the Wolves, all the Owllike Creatures, and all the other dark demons that do the Evil One's bidding. They will all be wiped out. Forever. When the time comes. But it is not yet time. We need to wait. We need to have hope. We need to be strong. We need to build our houses and our lives with bricks. Most importantly, we need to build up our houses and ourselves—with God's armor—which is God's Holy Word.

Only God can defeat the Darkness. Only God is the true Light. God is the true Light that illuminates the Darkness. God is the Word that will one day right the world with truth and Light.

We, God's people, wait in exile! We are in modern-day Babylon. Thousands of years ago, God carried his people into exile from Jerusalem to Babylon:

> *Build houses. Plant gardens. Marry and have sons and daughters. Increase in number. Seek peace. Pray to the Lord. Do not let the prophets and diviners deceive you. When seventy years are completed, I will come for you. For I know the plans I have for you. Plans to prosper you and not to harm you. Plans to give you hope and a future. I will bring you back from captivity. Jeremiah 29:5–14 (selected verses, paraphrased by author)*

The suffering and the dying had to come first for the exiles—before Day could come. Before God's people could understand what was not yet understandable.

CHAPTER 15

I consider that our present sufferings are not worth comparing with the glory that will be revealed in us. The creation waits in eager expectation for the sons of God to be revealed. For the creation was subjected to frustration, not by its own choice, but by the will of the one who subjected it, in hope that the creation itself will be liberated from its bondage to decay and brought into the glorious freedom of the children of God.

We know that the whole creation has been groaning as in the pains of childbirth right up to our present time. Not only so, but we ourselves, who have the first fruits of the Spirit, groan inwardly as we wait eagerly for our adoption, [as God's people], the redemption of our bodies. For in this hope we were saved. But hope that is seen is no hope at all. Who hopes for what one already has? But if we hope for what we do not yet have, we wait for it patiently. (Romans 8:18–25 NIV)

I HOPED THE JUDGE assigned by the court to hear my daughter's case would rule in her favor. I hoped Annie would be given custody of all her children, but I knew it might not work out that way. I had to be strong. I had to remember that there is much suffering in this life, but our suffering is nothing compared to what God's Son suffered on the cross. It is nothing compared to what his mother, Mary, suffered, at the foot of his cross. I needed to clothe myself with God's armor and wait for God's direction.

I needed to remember that suffering often comes before the rest. I needed to remember that suffering might come again and again. I needed to remember that God is always near—and that God is all I need.

Time was rapidly closing in. The trial was about to take place. Annie told me she had given all her documents and papers to her lawyer. She had given him information about her health issues, including her PTSD, her rheumatoid arthritis, her panic attacks, her Crohn's disease, and her depression and anxiety. She told him about the counselor she had been seeing on a regular basis during the past year, mainly because of her PTSD.

She told her lawyer about the local Safe House meetings she had been attending on a weekly basis because she feared that someone from the church might try to harm her or her children. She told him about the new school district in which she would be enrolling her children and that she would homeschool them if the children preferred that. She told him about the new safe house where she and the children would live. It was a good-sized house, and each child would have their own bedroom. She told him about the surrounding area and all that it had to offer the children. She googled all the information she could find about her future location and gave it all to her lawyer. She also told her lawyer that she would be near a number of extended family members who would help nurture the children.

She also gave her lawyer a copy of the Pretty Lady's manifesto, which listed all the rules of the "church" and punishments for breaking those rules. And Annie expressed fears for herself and her children if they continued to live close to the oppressive church she and her family had so recently escaped from.

Finally, she gave her lawyer seventeen years' worth of journals she had kept. She gave her lawyer everything she could think of to help him to build a case that the children should stay with her.

Her lawyer was fully armed with information from Annie! He also had all the information I had given him, which was quite damning toward the church and its leaders. She and her children needed to get away and start over fresh! At the same time, Annie knew that her children needed to spend some time with their father, and she was open to a generous visitation schedule.

Annie and I saw her lawyer one more time just prior to the court date. And with all of the information he had, I believed he would be confident in what he had to present to the court. However, he was hard to read. He would not talk to me—and he did not appear to be terribly confident. At all. In fact, he was still disheveled, out of breath, and distracted.

I said nothing to Annie, but I felt like I was wandering through Wonderland, hobbling parts of the way with a sharp pain in my side, alongside my friend Alice, the Queen of Hearts, a large White Rabbit hopping frantically about, and a terribly ugly looking Jabberwock, who spent most of his time smoking a strange-looking pipe and spewing out nonsensical advice to anyone who might listen.

Help us, Lord God. Whatever the outcome. Please help us.

That night, after Annie and I had met with her lawyer, I had a nightmare. The Prince of Darkness was back! In my dreams. Disguised as a woman! I didn't want to tell anyone my dream. Not yet! Besides, what would others think of me? Would they think my faith had become weak again? Would they think I now believed that God had abandoned me for a second time? Would they think I had been wrong about God in the first place—that God had never been there for me at all and that my belief about God helping me was just a fantasy or a fairy tale?

The nightmare happened in the Darkness between falling asleep at night and waking up to the light of a new day. I saw something. It was at the side of our bed. Next to my husband. I saw something wicked rise up, and I was immediately terrified.

It was a woman with a hard-looking face, wrinkled skin, short white hair, and shiny black eyes. She was looking right at me and smiling brightly. Too brightly. I thought she looked vaguely familiar, but in the next moment, I was sure I did not know her.

Suddenly, I heard screams! The screams were as sharp and shrill as a policeman's whistle! They were coming from deep inside of me, and they slashed through my body. The woman on the other side of the bed began to rise up higher. Then she reached over my husband and tried to touch me!

"Help me!" I screamed. "Something wicked is here! Help me!"

I felt someone shaking me hard. Is it the woman? Is this the end of me?

Then I heard my husband's voice. "Wake up, Sarah," he shouted. "Wake up! You are having a bad dream!"

And I tore my eyes from the space where I had seen the woman and looked into my husband's eyes. They were wide with fright, and his mouth was trembling. "It's over, Sarah," he said. "It is over!"

I let him hold me close, grateful for his presence. My heart slowed, my screams dissolved into nothingness, and I felt my body begin to relax. I took one more look. Was she really gone? I looked over and saw that the space by his side of the bed was empty. The woman was gone. It must have been a dream after all.

I fell into a restless sleep with my husband's arms wrapped around me.

It wasn't long before I woke up screaming again! The woman was back! She was reaching out to me once more! Stretching her arm over the bed toward my body. And my husband was not in the bed! *Where is he?*

Suddenly, the woman touched me! She touched me! One of her arms was on top of my arm! I tried to push it away, but her arm was too heavy! I could not push it away! I screamed! Wailed! Then my husband was back, and the woman disappeared. But this time, I had felt her! Her arm had been on top of my arm. I had felt it!

My husband comforted me once more and told me it was just a dream. I tried my best to believe him, but I did not go back to sleep that night. I kept vigil. I kept my eyes wide-open. I prayed. Thankfully, the woman did not return.

The next day, I had the feeling of being hunted. I could not rid the woman from my mind. And when night came, I told my husband I was afraid to go to sleep. In response, he prayed for the safety of both of us. He told me to go to sleep, resting in the knowledge that God's angels were watching over us. Before I closed my eyes, I looked over at the side of the bed and in all the corners of the room. Thankfully, I did not see her. Finally, exhausted, I went to sleep. It must have been a dream after all.

But was it?

Finally, be strong in the Lord and in his mighty power. Put on the full armor of God, so that you can take your stand against the devil's schemes. For our struggle is not against flesh and blood, but against the rulers, against the authorities, against the powers of this dark world and against the spiritual forces of evil in the heavenly realms. (Ephesians 6:10–12 NIV)

Lord God, please help me be brave. Help me remember that you are near me. Help me remember that you are all I need!

Being brave was difficult. A few days after having that frightening nightmare, I began to wonder if Annie's lawyer might be the real nightmare. I made myself stop that thought. That thought would be unkind. Unfair. I didn't really know him. He was not my lawyer after all. He was Annie's lawyer. Even if I thought he was doing very little for her. Even though I thought he was disheveled. And unorganized. And rude.

Still, I was very disappointed in him. I had given him a lot of information I thought might be useful for the trial, yet he had not made a single comment to me about any of it. Nothing positive. Nothing negative. Nothing at all. I wondered if he had even read what I had given him. But again, he wasn't my lawyer.

The last time we met with him, Annie gave him even more information. He took the new information and crammed it into his thick briefcase, which was already stuffed with all the medical documents Annie had given him, the research Annie had done on the school district where she would make her home, copies of all of Annie's journals she had kept during the time she had been in the church, and the names of people he could talk to who would vouch for her. His briefcase was filled with so many papers that he could barely close it, yet his only comment to Annie was that she had nothing to worry about. She would get the children. And then, after a very short time, he said he had all he needed, got up from his chair, and said that he had another appointment.

I felt sick inside as I left his office. Something was off. *Why is he so confident she will get the children?* I wasn't sure at all if Annie would get her children.

That night, I had another nightmare. That woman was after me again. However, this time, I knew who she was. She was the Prince of Darkness in disguise. I had seen her many times before, in other terrifying nightmares. In other terrifying forms.

In the dream, I was sitting in a chair, alone, in a gray room that was bare except for myself and the chair I was sitting in. I was tied up. My hands were tied. My feet were tied. I was tied to the chair. A cloth was wrapped around the lower portion of my face, covering my mouth. I tried to cry out for help, but only muffled sounds came from beneath the cloth. No one heard me.

It was then I realized no one would be coming for me.

I looked at my wrists. I thought I could wriggle out of the rope that bound them together, but I couldn't. I pulled and twisted to no avail. Sweat streamed out of my body from fear, exhaustion, and panic. I kept trying to scream, but very little sound came from beneath the cloth. No one heard me.

No one was coming for me.

I knew it was the haunting woman who had put me here. She had tied me up. She had covered my mouth with the cloth. She had left me in the room. Alone.

I was going to die!

I cried out from inside my head, "God!" I thought of Jesus, in the Garden, sweating rivulets of blood and calling out to his Father, "Not my will but your will be done."

I asked myself if I was ready to die, right then, in that place.

What happened next was miraculous. Immediately after crying out to God, the ropes fell away, and the cloth fell from my mouth. God had come for me! He had come to save me! God had heard my cry!

God had come for me!

It was not yet my time to die!

Time began to move quickly, and before we knew it, the first day of the trial arrived. Al and I, amazingly, were feeling somewhat hopeful as we entered the old courthouse. After all, Annie's lawyer had all the information he needed. What more could he possibly want? We believed he should be feeling self-assured and confident.

Annie was quiet, but she also seemed somewhat hopeful.

Annie's lawyer greeted me outside of the courtroom and told me to wait in the hallway while he went inside to find out if it would be possible for me to stand up for my daughter as a witness.

Fifteen long minutes later, he returned to the hallway to tell me I could not be a witness. In an instant, everything changed. Hope left Al and me. Our shoulders rounded. Our mouths went dry, and our hearts began to thump uncontrollably. *No! Oh no, this cannot be happening!* Annie's own mother could not vouch for her? Not one single person could vouch for Annie? This could not be happening! Not in America!

And yet, it was.

For the next hour or so, both lawyers briefly presented their cases and briefly questioned Bret and Annie. Before the march of the witnesses. And when the march began, witness after witness after witness came forward. And all of them spoke highly of Bret. (Even though, with the exception of the past year, they had not seen Bret for the twenty years before.)

One by one, the witnesses marched in. And one by one, they marched out. But no witness came for Annie. Not one. I was devastated.

And when the morning was over, we all quietly left the room. We did not march. We shuffled.

How could this be happening in America? And yet it was.

The afternoon of that first day in court, I saw four of Annie's children for the first time ever. I was standing in the hallway, and suddenly, Annie and Bret's kids appeared with a few of Bret's brothers and their wives. The children looked terrified: glassy eyes, pale faces, and backs rounded with fear. They stopped just a few feet from where I stood and huddled close together. They appeared to be longing for safety, for something familiar, for someone who would tell them that it was all just a dream and they could all go home.

When they saw me standing nearby, they absolutely froze. They were like statues: unmovable, cold, hard, lifeless. They had never in their lives seen me! All they knew about me was that I had been enemy number one on their church's list of enemies. For years! And as their enemy, they had been praying for my death for years! Now, here I was, standing right before them, in a giant hallway, in a giant courthouse, in a giant world, in the middle of a giant nightmare.

Their parents were splitting up, and the children did not know why. They did not know who to blame. They did not know who to be angry with. Now that I was standing before them, perhaps they wanted to blame me. Perhaps they wanted to believe I was the one who had ruined their lives.

Why not? After all, they had been taught that I was evil, and they had been taught to hate me for their entire lives.

And for what seemed to be the longest time, we all just stood and stared at one another. Not saying a word. Not knowing what to do next.

A bit later, mercifully, an official of the court, a woman, also came into the hallway. She began speaking with the children and gave them assurances that everything was all right. Then she led them into a small room where there was a long, wide table filled with food and drinks. Just for them. And I heard laughter from the children. They were feeling better.

What would come next for them? I knew they were each to meet with the judge, one by one, to tell her about their lives: their schools, their friends, their parents, some of their extended family members they had met, the things they liked to do, and so on. Only the oldest, Rory, was not present. He was scheduled to see the judge at a later time.

And so it was that they each went to see the judge in her chambers. One at a time. And as each of them finished their time with her, they made their way back to the room with all the food, all of them looking relieved and happy. All of them thinking it was over. It would all work out. Their lives would not change. The judge was a nice lady. Surely she would not make their lives change! And as they ate more food, laughed, and played around with each other in the little room, the court official told Annie and Bret what wonderful, happy, smart, and polite children they had!

And then, the children went home. And all was good.

But it wasn't really. I knew it was not good at all.

Holy Mary, Mother of God, how did you do it? Did you see the Wolf when it first came to your door? I would not blame you for an instant if you had not seen it. In the beginning, when children are new, what mother would allow herself to see a cunning Wolf dressed up in sheep's clothing knocking at her door? What mother would think that a gentle-looking lamb was hiding a murderous Wolf under its white wooly fleece? No mother would. It wouldn't happen.

It didn't happen to me either!

CHAPTER 16

THE SECOND DAY came, and it was time for everyone to go into the courtroom. Again. Annie and Bret had already taken their places with their lawyers up front. We took seats several rows behind Annie.

When it was time for Bret to take the stand for the second day, he began answering questions in a very slow and measured way. The questions were more complicated than they had been on the first day. Questions from his lawyer. And questions from Annie's lawyer. If I had a blindfold over my eyes, I would have thought Bret's measured way of speaking signaled that he was calm and collected, but he was not in the least bit calm—or collected. And I did not have a blindfold on. I saw his mouth was twisted in agony. His eyes were dark pools of pain. He appeared to be extremely rattled.

I was shocked at how thin he was, thinner than I had ever seen him. His entire appearance seemed to have changed from the confident Bret I had seen yesterday. He looked haggard, hollow, and far older than he really was. His hair looked dirty, matted with what looked like grease, slicked back off of his forehead. Hadn't he had time to clean up? Even his clothes looked unkempt—cheap-looking, rumpled, ill-fitting clothes. His shoes were worn and dull. I wondered if those were the best clothes he had. He appeared to be a totally defeated man. What had happened to the young strapping Bret I once knew and loved? What had happened since yesterday? Had I not noticed his appearance a day ago? Or had I been blind? Seeing only what I hoped I would see.

What had happened to the Bret who was so full of love and hope for the future? The handsome Bret who was so full of smiles and good will? He looked like a shell of his former self. What had the Pretty Lady in Fancy Robes done to him? What horrors had he seen inside that church? Participated in? Promoted? His face looked blank. Empty. It appeared as if his soul had been ripped away. He looked totally broken. What had they done to my son-in-law? What had that Dark Angel done?

Bret answered all the questions asked of him. And although some of his answers conflicted with what his witnesses had said the day before, all in all, he tried to answer as best as he could. He did a credible job. He did what he was supposed to do, all while his life was shattering right before him. Everything he had hoped for, dreamed about, and planned for was gone. Nothing would ever be the same. Nothing would ever be the same for any of us. I had so hoped, when Annie had first called me a few months ago, that we could all be one big happy family again. But it was not to be.

And then I realized more suffering would come. Before anything else could come. Before Daybreak. Before hope could show its face again. Suffering often came more than once. Sometimes again and again. But suffering could be followed by Day's face, for those who trusted in God. First the Darkness. Then the Light. Then the Darkness. Then the Light. Over and over again. It was just how life was on this side of heaven. It was just how life was when looking through a mirror, darkly.

I had finally come to know that God's people cannot escape suffering on this side of heaven. But there is hope for those who trust in God's plan for them. There is hope that Day's radiant face will come again. Between the sufferings. For a moment. Or for longer. For God is Day. And God is always near to us. Even in our sufferings. Even when we cannot see Day's face.

> *Now we see but a poor reflection as in a mirror; then we shall see face to face. Now I know in part; then I shall know fully, even as I am fully known. (1 Corinthians 13:12 NIV)*

After Bret finished answering a string of questions, another series of witnesses was called to the stand.

One by one, they entered the courtroom, each one slowly moving forward, as if about to meet their executioner.

Each one was sworn in and testified that Bret was a wonderful father and that his extended family would help him with the kids should the judge grant him custody of them.

And all I could think of was the fact that none of these witnesses really knew Bret. Just like the witnesses the day before, none of them knew anything about what had gone on inside that oppressive church. None of them really knew the horrors the children and their parents had endured—or participated in. None of them knew much of anything! They did not know Annie. They did not know any of the children. The only persons in that courtroom who did know some of the horrifying truths about what had taken place inside that church were my husband and me. And neither of us was asked—or permitted—to testify!

The Spiders were spinning furiously inside the courtroom. The Wolves were howling. And the Owllike Creatures were flying about, screeching while they flapped their wings and thrust out their razor-sharp talons.

After Bret and all his witnesses were questioned by both lawyers, there was a pause. No more witnesses came forward. Quiet filled the courtroom for a moment. On the surface, it appeared as if Bret and all his witnesses had done well on the stand.

And they had.

However, everything important had been left out of the witnesses' testimonies. Nothing Bret or his witnesses had said was altogether real. All of the questions from Bret's lawyer seemed to have been carefully crafted. Carefully controlled. And she, as well as all the witnesses, had carefully left out important facts. Every question was controlled. Every exhibit. Every witness. Every answer. Every objection.

And later, when it was time for Annie's lawyer to cross-examine Bret, even his concerns and occasional objections seemed controlled. Almost all his concerns and objections were overruled.

And while Bret's lawyer had plenty of witnesses and exhibits to show to bolster Bret's case, Annie's lawyer had nothing. No witnesses to counter what had been said. No exhibits to counter what the other lawyer had displayed. Nothing. He had no comments ready, no questions of any import. Nothing. And he did not use a single shred of any of the evidence from Annie—or from me—about what had gone on during the twenty years Annie and her family had been in captivity.

I wondered if all the precious information we had given Annie's lawyer was still in its original place—inside his overstuffed briefcase—or been destroyed. I believed Annie's lawyer had become a Wolf. Just like Bret's lawyer. As I looked around the courtroom, all I saw were Wolves' faces, their mouths salivating as they anticipated their kill.

They ... had won.

Annie … had lost.

It was a rousing performance for Bret's lawyer—and no performance at all from Annie's. Bret's lawyer's performance was almost too perfect, too smooth, and too contrived. It was as if the courtroom performance was the climax to a great many rehearsals. Bravo to Bret's lawyer! Rotten tomatoes to Annie's lawyer. How could Annie's lawyer have come to court so ill prepared? Or could it be that he played his part exactly the way it was intended? Had he been a part of all the dress rehearsals? Had the fix been in from the very beginning?

Nothing was as it seemed. The Wolves were in the courtroom, and it appeared as if no one could see them besides Al and me. And we couldn't say a thing. We couldn't do a thing about it.

Holy Mary, Mother of God, how did you do it? When you heard your Son accused of things he did not do. When you heard the crowds crying out to crucify him? When you saw him being led away to his death? How did you do it? Tell me, Mary, how did you do it?

When Annie took the stand, she, like Bret, tried her best to answer all the questions asked of her by both lawyers. But she was frequently prevented from answering fully. She was not allowed to elaborate or say anything at all regarding her former church. She was continually blocked by Bret's lawyer or overruled by the presiding judge.

Her own lawyer undermined her, and her case,

by saying little to nothing. He just let it all happen. Annie's lawyer had been hopelessly unprepared, outmaneuvered, and overwhelmed at every turn—or had he been a willing participant in a well-planned-out charade? Had he done anything at all to get ready? Had he read anything at all of what Annie and I had given him? It appeared as if he had done nothing.

On the stand, Annie had not been allowed to say anything about the church and the horrors she and her children had to endure as members. She had not been allowed to say anything about her husband's lack of attention and protection while they were members of that church. She had not been allowed to say anything about all the times her husband left her and the children in the hands of a violent and controlling leader. She had not been allowed to say anything about the fact that she had been a virtual prisoner in her own home for twenty years—and a virtual prisoner under the control of the church's leader for their entire marriage. And her husband had not put a stop to any of it!

She had not been allowed to talk about her anger toward her husband for not protecting her and their children for all those years. She had not been allowed to talk about her sessions with her therapist to work on her anger and her fears about the church, about the church leader, and about the lack of protection from her husband. She had not been allowed to talk about her sessions with counselors at the Safe House she visited weekly, about her fears for her life, or her fears for her children's lives. She had not been allowed talk about the curses she and the children had endured from church members or her fears of burning to death and going to hell if she spoke against the church. She had not been allowed to talk about the loss of her fifth child, "murdered" by the leader of the church, the Pretty Lady in Fancy Robes. And she had not been able to talk about how she had wished her husband would have stood up to that church leader and saved their child!

She had not been allowed to say one word about what had happened in that church and how that church had destroyed all of their lives. The judge told her that their years in the church were no longer relevant to their lives, and therefore, could not be spoken of.

Annie and I had given her lawyer plenty of information about their first twenty years of marriage ahead of time, so that he could speak up on her behalf, bring in witnesses, show exhibits, and explain how the church and its leaders had ruined Annie and Bret's marriage. However, he did not have one single exhibit or one single witness or one single strong word to say on her behalf. Nothing. I suspected her lawyer had been taken in by the Wolf.

Then came the point when Bret's lawyer and the judge essentially told Annie that nothing she could say about her first twenty years of marriage mattered in this courtroom. Nothing could be said about those years. None of her words about those years would be allowed. None of it counted. All those years were erased. The only thing that counted was the previous year of their marriage, the twenty-first year, the year after they left the church and began to live in the outside world. The kids seemed fine. They were smart, polite, happy, healthy, and doing well in public schools. Bret had tried to be a better father during the twenty-first year. He was home more. He helped out more.

And that was that. Nothing else mattered. The judge said she would make her decision solely on their twenty-first year of marriage.

CHAPTER 17

Where Is Justice? Where, O Lord, Is Justice?

T HIS IS WHAT the Lord says:

Maintain justice
And do what is right,
For my salvation is close at hand
And my righteousness will soon be revealed.
All who keep the Sabbath without desecrating it
And who hold fast to my covenant—
These I will bring to my holy mountain
And give them joy in my house of prayer.
Their burnt offerings and sacrifices
Will be accepted on my altar;
For my house will be called
A house of prayer for all nations.
—Isaiah 56:1, 6b–7 (NIV)

On the third day of the trial, Annie lost everything. She lost her husband. She lost her home. She lost most of her possessions. She lost financial support from her husband. She lost her children. She lost her soul. She lost everything.

At the end of the third day of the trial, the judge awarded all the children to Bret. Annie had no home, no means of financial support, no friends, and a very limited extended family that would be able to help her. She had nothing. And the children needed more than nothing. In contrast, Bret worked. Bret had a home, which was the only home the children had ever known. Bret had a vast array of extended family members who had pledged to help him out. And the children would stay in the same schools they had been enrolled in for the past year.

Bret got everything.

Annie lost everything.

And suffering once more filled me up. Would the suffering never end? Would Day ever show its face again—even for a moment?

Annie's anger raged. She had hoped to take the children out of state, to a Safe House, where they would all be secure. She had hoped to enroll them in good schools or homeschool them if they desired her to do so. She had hoped to get a job and help pay for some of the bills at the Safe House. She had hoped that her children would enjoy a new sense of freedom and safety far away from the horrors of what they had endured in that oppressive church. She had hoped that they would all begin brand-new lives and that they could be happy together.

But it was not going to happen!
She lost everything.
And they all got away with it:

- the judge
- the lawyers
- Bret
- Bret's extended family
- the Pretty Lady in Fancy Robes
- the members of the oppressive church
- the Spiders
- the Wolf
- the Owllike Creatures
- the Prince of Darkness himself

They had all won. They had been relentless! And they had all gotten away with it!

Yet all was not lost. God was near—and God heard the cries of his people. The suffering on that day was nearly over. Day was about to dawn. In God's time, Day would come! But none of us knew it.

The Prince of Darkness had been relentless in securing his prey.

Those of us fighting for and with Annie had been relentless in trying to rescue her and her family.

God had also been relentless.

And in the end, God would win. No matter how many sufferings any of us would endure on this side of heaven. In the end, God always prevails. He always saves those who genuinely trust and believe in him.

Sing praises to the Lord, O you his saints,
and give thanks to his holy name.
For his anger is but for a moment,
and his favor is for a lifetime.
Weeping may tarry for the night,
but joy comes with the morning.
You have turned for me my mourning into
dancing;
you have loosed my sackcloth
and clothed me with gladness,
that my glory may sing your praise and not be
silent.
O Lord my God, I will give thanks to you
forever.
—Psalm 30:4–5, 11–12 (ESV)

> *The Light shines in the Darkness, and*
> *the Darkness has not overcome it.*
> *—John 1:5 (ESV)*

Caption: Joy will come in the morning!
Attribution: Shannon Childress

The next three years were rough for all of us.

Bret remarried within a month or so after he won in court. Bret and the youngest children all moved into his new wife's home. Rory enlisted in the armed services, and the oldest daughter moved out of the house. The three younger children changed schools. They began making new friends.

Annie moved to a new state and soon formed a relationship with a young man she had known in her childhood. It was not long before she moved in with him. The children visited Annie and her boyfriend once a month. Annie found a full-time job working with women who had been abused by their boyfriends, husbands, fathers, or others. Most of the women she worked with were addicted to alcohol, drugs, or both. Many of them were victims of human trafficking.

Annie was very good at her job and related well to the women. She sought medical help for all her physical wounds and psychological help for all of her mental, emotional, and spiritual wounds.

Annie and her children spent some of their weekends with Al and me in our home. These weekends were difficult in many ways, but we welcomed them with wide-open arms.

The three youngest children exhibited various forms of depression, anxiety, and extreme anger. They seemed to have little understanding of what had happened to them and their family. They had few words to express their feelings, thoughts, questions, or anything else. The children have been, and still are, in counseling. They have all been doing well in public schools despite the horrendous experiences they all endured at the hands of their church's leadership.

Annie is doing well, although she is burdened with child support, which takes a significant portion of her income. She and her boyfriend have recently moved closer to the children. She is going to school full-time and is working full-time. She sees the children every other weekend. Al and I see Annie and her children frequently.

Bret is doing his best to be a good father. It has not been easy for him. He has been very kind to Al and me and has apologized for his role in bringing about all that happened during their twenty-year separation from the outside world. He has also apologized to his parents. He is extremely remorseful for his actions and his inactions. We have forgiven him and told him so. He lets us see the children when we are able.

The scars are still within all of us. The thorn in my flesh still pinches, but we will all be okay. God is with us. God is relentless. God is all we need. The Darkness and the suffering may come again, but Day always comes after for God's people. God promises.

Those who choose to trust in God all encounter suffering, but God is always near. God stays with his people. He helps his people. He guides his people. He shows his people how to help others who are suffering and do not understand what is not yet understandable.

If you love me, you will keep my commandments. And I will ask the Father, and he will give you another Helper to be with you forever, even the Spirit of Truth, whom the world cannot receive because it neither sees him nor knows him. You know him, for he dwells with you and will be in you.

These things I have spoken while I am still with you. But the Helper, the Holy Spirit, whom the Father will send in my name, he will teach you all things and bring to your remembrance all that I have said to you. Peace I leave with you; my peace I give to you. Not as the world gives do I give to you. Let not your hearts be troubled, neither let them be afraid. (John 14:15–17, 25–27 ESV)

And the story continues to unfold …

PART III

*Letters from Sarah to Her
Family and Close Friends*

LETTER 1

To Annie, our middle daughter,

I have said so much to you already, dear one. And I have written books with you inside of them. As if all the talking and all the writing will make all of those difficult times disappear.

But you and I both know that the memories of those years when you were gone will never completely fade. The years themselves have vanished. They were lost to all of us, but the memories will never vanish. They are seared into all our minds. Perhaps, in heaven, they will disappear. But then again, maybe it won't matter in heaven if they are still with us.

You lost everything during those years. Your freedom. Your dreams. Your aspirations. Your extended family. All your friends. Your husband. Your children. Your dignity. Your sense of self-worth. Your faith. Your God. Your very self. You lost everything. Including all those years. For they are now lost years. Never to be found again.

Your stepdad and I also lost those years. All those years. As did your siblings, your aunts and uncles, your cousins, your grandparents, your biological father, your stepmother, all of their children, your friends. Everyone who knew you and loved you. Your stepdad and I tried to get you away from your captors. But to no avail. You were kidnapped and held for twenty long years. And none of us can ever get those years back again.

The good news is that our time in heaven will last forever. And in comparison, the hurt of the lost years on earth will merely be a bump in the road. A blip on a screen. One tiny moment in time.

I wish it wouldn't hurt so much now! But it still does. And we all have to go on and live our lives as best as we can. Sometimes faring well. Sometimes not so well.

But if you should hear and understand anything at all from me, your mother, please hear and understand this: None of this is your fault. None of it! You were kidnapped. Brainwashed. Stolen from. Beaten down. Threatened. Forced to do things you would never do outside of your prison. None of this is your fault! Don't ever blame yourself for any of this, sweet girl.

You had to do whatever they told you to do. And you did. In order to protect your children. You stayed. In order to save them from total ruin. You remained. In order, one day, to bring them all out. And you did bring them all out, brave girl. You did, in time, with

God's help, bring them all out. Don't you ever forget that! None of your children may understand that now. But they will in time. You saved them. Thanks be to God!

All save one. You were not able to save your little son. Your leader took him from you. But that was not your fault either. And your son knows it. He knows how bravely you fought for him. And one day, you will see him again on the other side of this life. And you will be with him forever. Thanks be to God!

For now, dear heart, keep doing what you are doing. Love your children. And one day love your grandchildren. And after that, love your great-grandchildren.

And keep on going to school! Become that nurse you want to be! Help others! Physically. Mentally. Emotionally. Spiritually. You will have the opportunity to help so many. And you will. With God's help, you will.

And just one more thing, dear heart. Know that God loves you. Love God back! God will help you. Always.

I am so proud of you. And I so love you. As does your stepfather! Your stepfather and I could not love you more.

Mom

> *Go therefore and make disciples of all nations,*
> *baptizing them in the name of the Father and*

of the Son and of the Holy Spirit, teaching them to observe all that I have commanded you. And behold, I am with you always, to the end of the age. (Matthew 28:19–20 ESV)

LETTER 2

To my firstborn daughter,

I know this has all been difficult for you. Perhaps more difficult than I can ever know. The Dark Angel, disguised as a Pretty Lady in Fancy Robes, destroyed our family. We were all betrayed. All fooled. All taken in. And there is no way that we can reconstruct what was before the Dark Angel came. Our family was forever changed. And I know sometimes you weep inside because of it.

I do too. I weep for what was. I weep because you weep. And as a hen gathers her chicks under her wings, I wish I could gather you in my arms like I did when you were small. And wipe away your tears. But I can't. That time is long past. And we have all moved on. We have all survived.

I am so proud of what you have done with your injured life. Your wings no longer lay broken on the ground. They are strong and powerful. You have soared high. You have used all that once was broken and turned it into something beautiful.

Becoming a teacher and working with children is much more than I could ever have hoped for you. Helping others with broken wings is your passion. You know how much those damaged wings hurt. And you know how to mend them.

You were a beautiful squalling baby. And that was a good thing. All of that squalling became a powerful voice as you grew into a strong young woman. Strong enough to survive most anything. Strong enough to endure a wilderness of disappointment and loss. Strong enough to ask for help for your crippled wings. Strong enough to forge ahead with your life despite your brokenness.

I am thankful for all you are and for all that you have yet to become. Keep moving forward. Never give in to the Darkness. Never open the door to the Dark Angel. And remember that God is near to you. Always. And God is enough.

Love,
Mom

> *Surely he has borne our griefs and carried our sorrows; yet we esteemed him stricken, smitten by God, and afflicted. But he was wounded for our transgressions; upon him was the chastisement that brought us peace, and with his stripes we are healed. (Isaiah 53:4–5 ESV)*

LETTER 3

To my third daughter,

You are my youngest, and perhaps you have been hurt most by the Dark Angel. You were still at home when she came to our door. You were barely fifteen. And you could not have possibly understood what havoc the Dark Angel would bring when he came inside our house. I couldn't understand it either. For the longest time.

She came in disguise. And none of us knew what we had let in.

The Dark Angel stole your high school years from you. Those years should have brought you joy. You were about to become a young adult and then go out into the whole wide world. You were pretty, smart, and talented, but there was little joy in it for you as the Darkness inside our house grew ever darker—and then it smothered you.

I was not always there when you needed me. My mind was often on other things. And I was gone much of the time to see the police, lawyers, a private detective, a counselor, other parents who had children in the same group your sister belonged to, a family services organization, and even the FBI.

I was gone a lot. And you were left at home. Alone. Far too often. What must you have thought of me? How did you survive? How often did you stop your tears from falling, and instead, stuffed them inside?

And yet you did well with your schooling. I wish I had been there for you more often. For even when I was there physically, I was often absent emotionally. In a far-off land. Inhabited by a Pretty Lady in Fancy Robes. And Wolves, Black Skies, and Owllike Creatures screeching above, circling, waiting for the kill. And visions, nightmares, daymares, and shiny black Spiders spinning sticky webs.

I am amazed at who you are today despite your mother being absent much of the time when you were young.

Today, you work with youth who are difficult to work with and hard to love, yet you love them and help them grow into strong, caring adults. How were you able to survive, let alone help others in the world? How are you able to help those troubled children? Yet you do. Despite all the odds, you do.

How did you overcome the curse of the Dark Angel?

And yet you did. You did more than survive. You flourished! And today, you help those who need someone like you. You "get" what they need. You "get" how they feel. You "get" how to help them. And you absolutely amaze me. And I am so proud of you.

Keep doing what you are doing. And if your struggles helped you become who you are today, then that is what they were for. To make you stronger. More caring. More thoughtful. More wise. Keep on going.

And never look back to when I wasn't there for you. I did not know how much my absence was affecting you until you were gone.

Keep moving ahead, sweet girl. Don't take time to look back at the Darkness. It won't help you. It only wants to lure you back in.

I love you—and I always will. You will always be my youngest child. My baby. And I will always wish that things had been better for you in our house. Someday, I hope you will understand that suffering often comes before the Day. Before what is not understandable becomes understandable.

Never give up on any of your dreams, sweet daughter. And don't quit until all that you have planned for your life is done.

Always remember that God is near to you. And God is enough.

Love,
Mom

Then he said to Thomas, "Put your finger here, and see my hands; and put out your hand, and place it in my side. Do not disbelieve, but believe." Thomas answered him, "My Lord and my God!" (John 20:27–28 ESV)

LETTER 4

To our granddaughter/our fourth daughter,

You have always been dear to us. You, my sweet girl, filled a great hollowness inside our hearts after Annie left us. You brought us hope after the Dark Angel came and ruined our family. You brought us light when Darkness nearly swallowed us up. And you filled our days with laughter when it was difficult to form even a smile.

I wonder if you will ever truly understand how much you helped us heal and move forward, but it is okay if you don't. You don't need to understand it at all. Just know that we love you—and we will be forever grateful to you. That is enough.

Much of the sadness and pain we experienced over losing Annie faded when you were with us. You were our sun, moon, and stars when our days were otherwise bleak, sunless, and devoid of any skylights at all.

Holding onto your little hand lifted our spirits.

Taking you to school each morning gave purpose to our lives. Watching you grow and learn at school and at home was our great joy. And taking you to church for worship was glorious.

You were wise beyond your years. I came to believe that perhaps you possessed an old soul: thoughtful, caring, and good. And I will never forget the words you said to me on one of my darkest days as I was writing about Annie in my journal: "Don't give up, Grandma. Never ever give up. Don't quit! Don't quit until it is done."

You were only eight years old when you uttered those words to me. I have never forgotten them. And whenever I feel I just can't go on anymore, I remember your words. And those words help me get through a day. Or two. Or more. I believe God spoke to me through you on that day.

Do you remember your time with us? Do you remember the things you said to me? Do you remember how I rocked you in the middle of the night when you cried out with fear? A fear you were unable to explain to me? A fear you have most probably forgotten all about?

Do you remember going to church with us? You and your doll and your purse full of paper and colored pencils? Do you remember the time you got up from your seat during a choir song, put your little hands over your ears, and called out, "Stop! You are too loud! You are hurting my ears!"

Do you remember all the swim practices we took

you to? How you struggled learning to dive? Do you remember how proud we were of you when you started winning races at your swim meets?

Do you remember playing with your friend down the street? Do you remember how you girls loved your American Girl dolls? How you loved riding your bikes around our cul-de-sac? And how you loved all the sleepovers at your friend's house?

Do you remember singing in your spring concerts at school? Grandma and Grandpa sitting in the bleachers and cheering you on? Always nearby whenever you needed us?

Then you became a middle school student, and soon after that, a high school student. And we continued to sit in the bleachers, cheering you on at all your events.

Thank you for helping us, dear girl. Thank you for filling us up with your love when we most needed it. Thank you for allowing us to care for you during your growing-up years. You saved us. You absolutely saved us when we did not understand the suffering we had to endure. When we did not understand what was not yet understandable in our lives. We will be forever grateful for you. You were and are a gift sent by God, sent to us to help mend our weary spirits.

And now, on the brink of full womanhood, please don't ever forget the words you gave to me so long ago. And don't forget the words I give back to you today: "Never give up, sweet girl. Never ever give up. Don't quit. Don't quit until it is done."

Always remember that we, your grandparents, will stay near to you. For as long as we can. And God will stay with you for your entire life after we are gone. Always leave a part of your heart open for God to live in, sweet girl. God wants to live with you. And God is all you need. God is always all you ever need. We love you so much!

Grams and Pop Pops

> *Sing praises to the Lord, O you his saints, and give thanks to his holy name. For his anger is but for a moment and his favor is for a lifetime. Weeping may tarry for the night, but joy comes with the morning. (Psalm 30:4–5 ESV)*

LETTER 5

To our youngest grandson,

I was with your mom a lot when she carried you in her womb. She had already miscarried babies. I think she was afraid she would lose you too. She did not want to be alone.

Shortly before you were born, I stayed with your mom for a time and helped care for your older sister.

When your daddy arrived home after work each day, your mom would completely relax. Her shoulders would straighten up. The lines on her face would become softer. And the frantic look in her eyes would subside.

Poor Mama. She was so terrified of losing you.

And then one day, you decided it was time to be born. And after a very long labor and subsequent C-section, there you were. Pink. Good sized. Squalling. And ready to eat.

And fear totally left your mama. At the same time, fear entered me. Here you were. And you were so perfect and beautiful. But were you really here? Or were you but a dream. A dream that would soon vanish.

Now I was the one who was terrified! I had lost so many grandchildren. The six children Annie had given birth to. My oldest daughter's two miscarriages. (Which, in coming years, would become a total of five miscarriages.)

Yet here you were. A miracle. And just like that, Daddy put you in my arms while Mama rested for a while. And you looked up at me and seemed to say, "Grandma, don't worry. I am here. I am here to stay! I won't ever leave you!"

And somehow, I believed you. But I did not know if I could love you. What if you were wrong? What if you left us? I was not sure I could trust my heart to love you. And risk more loss. But I could hold you. And I could help take care of you when you and your mama came home. When Daddy was at work. I could do that and protect my heart at the same time. I could do that. I simply would not give my heart to you. I couldn't. I was too afraid.

I stayed in your house for six weeks. Or maybe it was more. I can't recall. But I can recall all the activity in your house during that time! Making meals. Helping your mama to the bathroom. Doing laundry. Folding clothes. Some of those clothes were yours! And I would marvel at the smallness of them. How could they be so tiny? How could there be such a tiny person living in this house?

And the diapers! How could you go through so many diapers in a day? And there was dishwashing. And bottle drying. (Even though you took most of your nourishment from your mama.)

Other times, when I was at your house, I would take your sister to school in the morning. And pick her up from school in the afternoon. And I became friends with other grandparents who were either picking up or delivering their grandchildren. And parents too. And school staff. Especially those at the big front desk near to the entrance where your sister and I walked in and out each day.

And I would help Mama rock you if Mama wasn't feeling well. Or help your sister with her homework. Or give her after-school snacks. Or whatever else she needed.

And soon your mama was able to take care of both you and herself. I did not have to help her every day. At that point in time, I had not given my heart to you. Your sister had it. Only your sister.

But, somehow, you grabbed it when I wasn't looking. You grabbed my heart! And I was surprised that there was still enough left over for your sister. I found out there was plenty enough for both of you. And I realized I was no longer afraid. It was all going to be okay. Be still my heart! I had room for both! And my heart rejoiced. It was a brand-new day! I was no longer afraid!

And before I knew it, you were two. And your mama decided to go back to work. But who was going to take care of you? Me, I hoped. And I asked Mama if I could take care of you, and Mama said yes. I was very happy. You were happy too, and we had great times together.

Some days it was dark and rainy outside, and we watched our favorite shows on TV: *Thomas and Friends, Blaze, Peppa Pig, Paw Patrol,* and *Max and Ruby. Max and Ruby* was our very favorite for a while. You would laugh and laugh! And you loved *The Wiggles* as well. And sometimes, you would fall asleep while you were watching one of your shows. I would fall asleep too—right beside you.

And sometimes we would get out the gigantic blocks that Grandpa had as a little boy. And you built roads and towers for your cars. And as you grew into three and then four, you had more and more cars to play with, and you made more and more elaborate structures with those blocks!

Sometimes, when it was nice outside, we would take our dogs for a walk. As we walked, we had a wonderful time counting mailboxes, trash cans, fire hydrants, and anything else you wanted to count. And you would point out letters and numbers you eyed on people's mailboxes.

When you were in kindergarten, I helped your teacher in your classroom. When you were in first grade, you would read me books from the library— and then you were second grade, and then third.

And I sat with you every day after school until

your mama got home from work. Unless you went to one of your friend's houses.

And now you are growing up fast, and I don't stay with you so much. You get off the school bus and go into your house alone. Your sister gets home a few minutes later. You get your own snacks. Do your own homework. Build intricate objects with your Legos. Play with all of your devices. And many evenings, you are out playing baseball with Daddy.

You are a busy boy. But not too busy yet to want to spend time with your grandma and grandpa. That will come in a few more years.

Know that Grandma and Grandpa love you and always will. I am so thankful that we have been able to spend time with you. You made our hearts sing.

Love,
Grandma

> *When I was a child, I spoke as a child, I understood as a child, I thought as a child: but when I became a man, I put away childish things. For now we see through a glass, darkly; but then face to face: now I know in part; but then shall I know even as also I am known. (1 Corinthians 13:11–12 KJV)*

LETTER 6

To Annie's children

I never saw your births. I never took care of you. I did not know most of your names. I did not know the color your eyes. Or what you liked to do. Or anything at all.

I knew each of you existed. I knew how many boys there were. And how many girls. I knew one of you died at birth.

That was all. I knew nothing else.

And over the years, how I longed to see each one of you, hold each one of you, help take care of each one of you. But it was not allowed. There were six of you counting the baby who died. I was never allowed to have communication with any of you.

And how I grieved. Every hour of every day, week, month, and year. You were always in my mind and on my lips as I uttered my pleas to God to keep you all safe.

And every night, I prayed this prayer:

Now I lay *them* down to sleep.
I pray Thee Lord *their* souls to keep
And if *they* die before *they* wake,
I pray Thee Lord *their* souls to take.
(adapted from Joseph Addison's "Now I Lay Me Down to Sleep")

That was the only hope I ever had to see you. On the other side. With God. In heaven.

And that is the way it was for years and years. Until five of you came out of captivity: one who was post high school, three high schoolers, and one junior high student.

Your grandpa and I have loved you. Wept for you. And prayed for you.

For years. And years. Until we finally met you. And today, we love you and pray for you still. And we are thankful for how well you are all doing. We are also thankful that you are all in our lives today.

It has been quite a journey. But God is good. God answered our prayers. And we are so grateful!

Love,
Grandma

> *Blessed be the God and Father of our Lord Jesus Christ, the Father of mercies and God of all comfort, who comforts us in all our affliction, so that we may be able to comfort those who are in any affliction, with the comfort with*

which we ourselves are comforted by God. For as we share abundantly in Christ's sufferings, so through Christ we share abundantly in comfort too. (2 Corinthians 1:3–5 ESV)

LETTER 7

A Letter to My Parents

Dear Mother and Father,

I wish you both could be here today so I could tell you the news. Your granddaughter, Annie, has come home.

You never had a chance to see her again after she left us all those years ago.

After you both passed, I mourned for you. Not only because you were gone, but because you never had a chance to say goodbye to Annie.

Was Annie on your mind as you left this earth? Did you mourn for her? Did you mourn for her child? Did you mourn for the rest of your family struggling with Annie's disappearance?

I guess I just want to tell you today that she is home. She and five of her children are home. The children are nearly grown, and they are adjusting to the new world they now find themselves in. But they are home. All save a baby who died at birth.

And I ask you, "Have you seen her baby? Her little son? Do you visit with him? Play with him? Rock him? Has he been able to tell you his story? Does he sing with the angels? What color are his eyes?"

For years, I did not know the color of any of Annie's children's eyes. Now, I do. For years, I did not even know their names. Now, I do. They all have beautiful eyes—blues, browns, and greens—and they all have beautiful names as well.

We are still in the early stages of their coming back into our world, so it is an adjustment for us as well. But we are figuring it out. It will take time.

I miss you both so much. We all do. I hope somehow you can know what I am writing to you today. It would mean so much to me and the rest of the family as well if we knew you knew.

I love you! Someday we will all be together again. At the feet of God. Someday I will have the chance to rock Annie's baby boy, the one she lost at birth. And someday we will be able to hold hands as we walk a short distance to welcome other loved ones who will come.

Until then, remember me. I will always remember you.

Your daughter,
Sarah Elizabeth Rose

> *Behold! I tell you a mystery. We shall not all sleep, but we shall all be changed, in a moment, in the twinkling of an eye, at the last trumpet. For the trumpet will sound, and the dead will be raised imperishable, and we shall be changed. (1 Corinthians 15:51–52 ESV)*

LETTER 8

To My Extended Family

Dear ones,

I am not sure if any of you truly understand what happened to Annie and her family. How they suffered. How I suffered. How my husband and my other children suffered.

Sometimes it is easier not to understand. I know. I was there for a while myself—in the beginning. I had not realized, in the beginning, that it was evil that was causing most of it. Evil. For a number of years, I had not understood it. I had not believed it. Evil happened to other families. Not my family.

But I was wrong. It did happen. To my family. And to some of those who tried to help us. It happened. The Prince of Darkness came to our door. And we let him in. And before we knew it, he was running rampant in our lives.

And we were all nearly destroyed.

Looking back, at the beginning, I was upset that you did not understand what was happening to us. To Annie. To her family. To me. To my husband. Somehow, I thought if you could just understand it, you could somehow make it all go away.

I know now that neither you—nor anyone else—could have made it go away. Who would have understood it? It was too unbelievable. Too otherworldly. Who would have understood it? Not many. Perhaps not more than a handful.

And so, I accepted the fact that it was just too hard for you to understand. And I decided, that despite the uncomfortableness and frustration I sometimes felt toward you, I loved you anyway. And I knew you loved me back.

You, dear ones, are my family! The only family I have! I share no other blood ties outside of you. How could I ever let my uncomfortableness and frustration get in the way of that? I could not. I will not.

And so I pray that one day you will understand. And I pray that one day you will believe. And I pray that one day you will rejoice that Annie and her family are home.

And now, dear ones,
The Day is here,
The old Day has faded,
And a new Day is upon us.
They have all come home!
But it is still too hard for you,

To understand.
It is still too hard for you,
to believe what happened.
Maybe,
it will be that way,
Forever.
You are my family,
And I am your daughter/sister.
I love you all, dear ones,
And I know that you love me as well.
Someday you will see clearly.
But now we can only look through a glass darkly.
Someday,
You will wipe away Annie's tears.
Someday, we will all understand everything.
Until then,
We will love each another,
And we will move on
As best we can.
—Sarah E. Rose

I will lead the blind by ways they have not known, along unfamiliar paths I will guide them; I will turn the Darkness into light before them and make the rough places smooth. These are the things I will do; I will not forsake them. (Isaiah 42:16 NIV)

LETTER 9

To Other Parents Who Have Lost Their Children to Oppressive Groups

Dear ones,

Most of you understand that your children are caught under the power of a person or persons who want to control them. They are holding your children captive. Physically. Mentally. Emotionally. Spiritually. They hold absolute power over your children. They are relentless. They hold on to your children with threats of harm, even death. They are evil. Truly evil. They spin webs of Darkness and deceit. They are Dark Angels with one goal. They want to devour your children's souls.

Some of you have children who have physically escaped their prisons, but they are still struggling in ways that are difficult for you to grasp. And even though you rejoice at the fact that they are no longer physically held captive, you grieve for them as they struggle, trying to adjust back into the worlds they left behind.

And you weep for them as you think about the lost years. You weep for yourself as well. And you wonder if your world will ever be righted again. You wonder if things will ever be as they once were. You grieve what is forever gone.

I get it. But I also believe our worlds have a chance to be righted once more, in time. Things will never be what they once were. Never. But we can still go on with our lives. I struggle. I always will struggle, but I choose to go on with my life.

My world stands upright most days now. And all of the skylights are back in their places. But things will never be the same. The lost years are forever lost. My heart will always carry a heaviness in it.

Unfortunately, we will continue to revisit that broken world, that place of drought and sorrow, over and over and over again as we journey forward. Still, we can go forward.

We must never give up hope. Our spirits can all be restored. Perhaps our children's spirits will one day be restored as well.

The Lord is close to the broken-hearted and
saves those who are crushed in spirit.
—Psalm 34:18 (NIV)

Your friend in Christ's sufferings,
Sarah E. Rose

ACKNOWLEDGMENTS

WITH MUCH THANKS to many friends and colleagues who shared their artistic talents with me while I kept you updated on my progress in writing this volume. I especially want to express my deep appreciation to Shannon Childress, Marjatta Heinonen, Donna Lark, and Kris Stoyer for the use of their works. Their images give powerful expression to my words.

Thanks to my husband who read and reread this manuscript and gave me suggestions when necessary. He never gave up believing in this manuscript. He never quit. Until it was done.

Thanks also to all those from WestBow and LifeRich, who worked with me and prepared my manuscript for publication. It has been slow and laborious for all of us.

But it is done. None of us gave up. None of us quit. Until it was done. And it is now done!

Most of all, thanks be to God who is gracious and merciful and allows us to build houses and dream dreams wherever we find ourselves. Even while in exile. Even while the Prince of Darkness is trying to destroy us. God will never let us be destroyed if we look for our strength in him. And only in him.

Soli Deo Gloria.